# The Best Saturdays of Our Lives

D1713492

# THE BEST
## Saturdays of Our Lives

MARK MCCRAY

# THE BEST SATURDAYS OF OUR LIVES

*iUniverse books may be ordered through booksellers or by contacting:*

*iUniverse*
*1663 Liberty Drive*
*Bloomington, IN 47403*
*www.iuniverse.com*
*1-800-Authors (1-800-288-4677)*

*Because of the dynamic nature of the Internet, any web addresses or links contained in this book may have changed since publication and may no longer be valid. The views expressed in this work are solely those of the author and do not necessarily reflect the views of the publisher, and the publisher hereby disclaims any responsibility for them.*

*Any people depicted in stock imagery provided by Thinkstock are models, and such images are being used for illustrative purposes only. Certain stock imagery © Thinkstock.*

*ISBN: 978-1-4917-5508-2 (sc)*
*ISBN: 978-1-4917-5507-5 (e)*

*Library of Congress Control Number: 2015900979*

*Print information available on the last page.*

*iUniverse rev. date: 09/19/2018*

# DEDICATION

To everyone who was instrumental in creating and building the competitive kids' television business.

To my dear wife, Joy, whose unwavering support of my television career was wonderful. I know she's smiling at me and the family from heaven.

To my sons, Jomar and Miles McCray, and my partner, Ron Jones, for their love, laughs, and support. I would also like to thank God for his many blessings.

# CONTENTS

# PREFACE

I believe that the Bronx, New York, was perhaps one of the best places for me to grow up, because New York gave me access to plenty of wonderful television programs. The New York market featured the big three networks—CBS, ABC, and NBC—but the market also included three independent stations—WWOR (channel 9), WPIX (channel 11), and WNEW (channel 5). This meant that I was able to see a variety of syndicated animation and live-action shows during the week, including the pre-1948 *Looney Tunes* cartoons; *Casper the Friendly Ghost*; *Felix the Cat*; *Captain Scarlet and the Mysterons*; *The Marvel Super Heroes*; *Gigantor*; *Courageous Cat and Minute Mouse*; *Mr. Magoo*; *Batfink*; *The Thunderbirds*; *The Little Rascals*; and *Wonderama*, a live-action variety show hosted by Bob McAllister that was broadcast on Metromedia-owned stations, including WNEW in New York.

Like most kids, I looked forward to watching Saturday morning television, and I didn't pay much attention to creative changes until one Saturday morning. I thought I was just watching another Superman cartoon, but I almost fell off the couch when I saw Superman show up with Green Lantern, the Atom, the Flash, and Hawkman, who came together as the Justice League of America! The cartoon, titled "Bad Day on Black Mountain," was my first introduction to the other superheroes of the DC universe. In addition, more wonderful television surprises were on the horizon. During the same championship season (1967–1968), I watched the *Space Ghost* crossover episodes that featured Space Ghost meeting the Herculoids, Mightor, and the genie Shazzan. It was very cool to find out that Space Ghost and the other great heroes existed in the same universe.

By the time I was nine years old, I was reading comic books as well as looking forward to the new Saturday morning cartoons that premiered every September. During the summer of 1970, I was sent to day camp and met a guy named Gerald, who would change the way I looked at television forever. Gerald and I shared the same interests—cartoons and comic books. However, Gerald also knew all the players, including Hanna-Barbera Productions, Filmation Associates, Sid and Marty Krofft Productions, Rankin-Bass Productions, and DFE (DePatie-Freleng Enterprises), which I would later call the Big Five. By the '80s, I would call the group the Big Seven with the addition of Ruby-Spears Productions and DIC Enterprises. These were studios that consistently produced television shows for Saturday morning programming.

When the new television season started during the fall of 1970, I started reading credits and familiarizing myself with all the Saturday morning players as well. *Josie and the Pussycats* was an early influence. I didn't think the series was going to be any good, mainly because Filmation Associates had already produced the comic-to-cartoon adaptations of *The Archies* and *Sabrina the Teenage Witch*, and while *Josie and the Pussycats* originated from the same comic book publisher, I didn't think there was anything special about Josie. I was blown away by the direction Hanna-Barbera took with *Josie and the Pussycats*. Instead of the usual teenage fluff and romances that were prominent in the *Josie* comic book series, Josie and her friends became the kids who were in the wrong place at the wrong time, rose to the occasion, and saved the day. The fact that an African American singer (Patrice Holloway) sang the opening theme song was also inspiring and gave me goose bumps! The late '60s and early '70s was the era of bubblegum music, and *Josie and the Pussycats* brought a great, new soulful sound to Saturday morning television.

By middle school, I was following the adventures of the live-action *Shazam!* television series, which featured the character Billy Batson (actor Michael Gray) saying the word *Shazam* and turning into the grown-up hero Captain Marvel. Jackson Bostwick played Captain Marvel in season one, and John Davey played Captain Marvel in seasons two and three. I was so inspired by *Shazam!* that I sent a pitch to Filmation Associates, the studio that produced the series, which resulted in an autographed picture of the *Shazam!* cast and a nice letter from Sherry Carter (the studio secretary) explaining that the Filmation could not accept unsolicited material.

In 1988, I sent Filmation Associates (later known as Filmation Productions) another letter, this one congratulating the studio on their release of their full-length feature *Pinocchio and the Emperor of the Night*. To my surprise, Arthur Nadel, executive vice president of production, responded. This encouraged me to send Filmation a pitch for new show ideas.

During July of 1989, my wife, Joy, and I booked a trip to LA for a vacation and to hang out with our friends John and Denise Johnson, who lived in Manhattan Beach. John and I worked together at Dun and Bradstreet, and he had recently relocated to the West Coast. In addition to reuniting with old friends, I had also secured an interview with Lou Scheimer, who was the president of Filmation Productions. Lou had received my pitch a few months back and was impressed with the pitch materials.

I grew up watching and enjoying many of his cartoons and live-action productions, which included *The Archies* and *He-Man and the Masters of the Universe*. Joy and I borrowed Denise's car and drove to the Valley, where Filmation Productions were located. Lou's secretary, Joyce Loeb, had only booked a half-hour appointment, and when Lou wanted to see my wife and me together, my hopes for a job were dashed because Lou didn't want to talk to me solo.

However, we had a great conversation, and Lou smiled at me and said, "You know more about my shows than I do, and I produced the shows." The half-hour appointment turned into a two-hour meeting, with Lou sharing stories and anecdotes about his many years working in the industry. After our meeting, Lou offered Joy and me a ride back to Manhattan Beach. While Lou's company wasn't hiring, he was impressed with all the Filmation information I had sent him, and he encouraged me. He said, "This is great information. You need to find a way to get it out there."

So as Joy and I flew back to New York, I thought about his words and thought to myself that instead of focusing on just one studio contact, why not send information to the entire animation community? In the fall of 1992, I decided it was time to launch my Saturday morning newsletter, titled *The Best Saturdays of Our Lives*. The goal of the newsletter was to bring attention to the origins of competitive programming trends, the classic television series, as well as the current trends of kids' television. My friend Cheryl Johnson-Watts, whom I worked with at Group W Cable (now known as Time Warner Cable), was working at Nickelodeon, and she gave me many contact names for the newsletter.

After a few months of sending out the newsletter, I started getting responses; Linda Simensky (director of animation for Nickelodeon) sent me a note, followed by Mike Lazzo, who had recently launched Cartoon Network (he was the network's vice president of programming). Joe King (executive vice president of Sid and Marty Krofft Productions) called me personally to thank me for my review of *H. R. Pufnstuf*. I also had the mentoring ear of Arthur Nadel, who worked alongside Lou as creative director in charge of production.

I became friends with Bob Rozakis, the executive director of production at DC Comics, who also doubled as the company's answer man. He invited me to participate and supply cartoon trivia during his Internet show. We had a great time, and some of my questions really threw the audience.

I was encouraged to keep sending out the newsletters and received notes from Joe Mazzuca (the executive in charge of production at Hanna-Barbera) and Bob Glazer (the president of American Film Technologies, a company that transformed black-and-white films to color films). By 1996, Cartoon Network invited me to film a pilot titled *This Week in Cartoons*, hosted by Seth MacFarlane (the creator of *Family Guy*). The pilot also featured Linda Simensky (whom I finally met in person). *This Week in Cartoons* featured Seth, Linda, and me as talking heads debating our favorite cartoon shows. We shot the pilot on the *Larry King* set at CNN in New York and had a great time filming it. It was a pleasant experience, and I felt so blessed to be able to participate in such a great project.

While the pilot didn't go anywhere, one of the producers I met on the set, Kaili Rubin, told me that there might be some freelance opportunities in Atlanta, where Cartoon Network is headquartered, and since my wife wanted to move to Atlanta, it was a no-brainer to move down south.

I had to wait almost two years before I could secure a job with Cartoon Network since there were no openings, but in June of 1998, Kaili Rubin came to my rescue again when she gave me a tip about a position with the Cartoon Network library. I secured an interview with Dick Connell and Marvetta Fields. The interview went great, since they were looking for a "cartoon expert."

After I secured the library position, I reported to Marvetta, who would mentor and help me secure a position with the Boomerang network a few months prior to the network's launch.

*The Best Saturdays of Our Lives* was originally published from 1992 to 1996 and was sent out on a monthly to bimonthly basis to a list of animation studios, television networks, and various comic book publishers. Some of the newsletters selected for this book have been edited, while other newsletter episodes have been combined for the purpose of consistency. There are also gaps in the newsletter numbering because some of the newsletters did not make the final cut for creative reasons. However, the newsletters that were selected for the book edition of *The Best Saturdays of Our Lives* represent a comprehensive history of the world that was created when Saturday morning television discovered how to be creative, competitive, and innovative. That is what I consider to be the big bang!

# ACKNOWLEDGMENTS

Special thanks to Van Partible; Tom Tataranowicz (Gang of 7 Animation/Tom T.Animation); Bob Beasley and Kim Campbell Beasley (Paws, Inc.); Julie Heath and Lisa Fitzgerald (Warner Bros.); Fred Ladd (Greatest Tales Company); Alex Segura (Archie Comics, Inc.); Patricia Coddington (Cartoon Network); Brian Jones (DreamWorks Animation); and the iUniverse editors and staff. I would also like to thank Zachary White (Adult Swim) for his friendship and support; and Taylor Johnson (Adult Swim) whose great artistry brought the original book concept cover to life.

I would also like to acknowledge the wonderful people who supported the original newsletter, including Donovan Cook; Lou Scheimer; Arthur Nadel; Kaili Rubin; Mike Lazzo; Linda Simensky; Joe King; Bob Rozakis; Robby London; Joe Mazzuca; Bob Glazer; Darryl McCray; Rodney McCray; Barry Mills (The Rudy and GoGo World Famous Cartoon Show); and Cheryl Johnson-Watts. Lastly, I want to recognize the PR professionals who provided the images for the original newsletter printing: Sarah Baisley (Film Roman); Carol Raverner (Alliance Communication Corporation); Carol Keis (Hanna-Barbera); Tom Brocato and Kate Chester (MCA Television); and Bill Wright (Nickelodeon). Special mention to the wonderful Noelle Brown (Pryor Associates) and Elissa Johansmeier (FOX and Pryor Associates), who not only went above and beyond to make sure I received images for the original newsletter, but also sent personal notes of support.

# INTRODUCTION

The fall of the 1966–1967 television season was just supposed to be another year of great entertainment from the big three networks—CBS, NBC, and ABC. While prime-time newcomers like *Star Trek* (NBC) were going up against veteran shows, such as *My Three Sons* (CBS), the big story of the 1966–1967 season was happening on Saturday morning with the debut of *The New Adventures of Superman* (CBS).

Green-lit by a young programming executive named Fred Silverman, *The New Adventures of Superman* quickly catapulted from CBS's third-place Saturday morning schedule into first place. Of course, one television network beating a competing network wasn't big news. However, *The New Adventures of Superman* ratings numbers proved to reluctant advertisers that huge revenues could be achieved on Saturday morning programming.

Prior to the 1966–1967 season, animated comedies ruled the ratings roost on Saturday morning, but the action-adventure show *Superman* proved to be a big game changer and brought Saturday morning programming into its own as a viable revenue-generating business. The entire programming phenomenon was truly the big bang of Saturday morning television.

Fred Silverman received his first big promotion during this period, and over the years he would define for a generation the role of the modern television programmer.

The fledging Filmation Associates studio that coproduced *The New Adventures of Superman* with DC Comics became firmly established during the 1966–1967 season and joined an elite group of studios that consistently produced Saturday morning programming during the '60s, '70s, and '80s. That group included Hanna-Barbera Productions,

1

Rankin-Bass Productions, DePatie-Freleng Enterprises, and—a few years later—Sid and Marty Krofft Productions.

When studios sold series to networks, the networks would typically order fifteen to eighteen episodes. However, if the series did not achieve high ratings, the network would not order new episodes for the second season. Mid-high ratings would result in a half order (five to eight episodes), while super high ratings would result in a full episode order for the second season. Of course, these rules were not always fair, as network politics at times played a part in which shows or studios got the better deal.

Lou Scheimer told me there was a practice of quid pro quo, which required studios to make a requested show for the networks, and in turn the networks would buy a series from the studios. However, there were times the studios benefited from the networks as well. The origins of the first animated *Sabrina the Teenage Witch* series came about when Fred Silverman was on vacation in the French Rivera and called Lou Scheimer and instructed his studio to acquire the rights to *Sabrina the Teenage Witch*, which became the sensation of the 1969–1970 season.

The studios would stay open for six months and crank out the episodes, and after the episode orders were complete, the studios would lay everyone off for six months until the next cycle. However, during the '80s, first-run syndication (non-network) programming kept the studio's doors open all year long. The industry today is vastly different. Networks own their own studios and create their own programming as well as opt to acquire or cofinance new potential series from independent producers.

Throughout the book, I will take you through the journey of television trends, programming, and series reviews and illustrate how the big bang of the 1966–1967 season has connections through the decades.

During the 1966–1967 season, *The Marvel Super Heroes*, which was syndicated, was produced with a budget of $6,000 per cartoon, with three cartoons airing per episode, while *The New Adventures of Superman* was produced with a budget of $36,000 per episode. However, the going rate during the 1966–1967 season was actually $45,000 per episode for established studios such as Hanna-Barbera. Thanks to the game-changing events of the 1966–1967 season that propelled CBS's Saturday morning into the top spot, at the start of the 1967–1968 season, all the broadcast networks were eager to get superheroes on their respective schedules.

Filmation Associates and Grantray-Lawrence Productions benefitted by getting increased budgets and staff. The creative teams proved that even with limited resources, wonderful animated moments could be achieved, even if those moments were not necessarily consistent. ABC television signed deals with Marvel Publications, Inc., which gave the network the perfect competitive edge against CBS, which was loading up *The Superman/Aquaman Hour of Adventure* for its 1967–1968 debut. NBC created its own superheroes, including *Birdman and the Galaxy Trio* (Hanna-Barbera) and *Super President* (DePatie-Freleng Enterprises). Advertisers like Kellogg's created custom billboards and advertising for some of the high-rated superhero programming.

Saturday morning was growing and evolving. The networks were trying out new genres as well as borrowing strategies from prime-time television. Music was becoming a major influence, as well as a Great Dane named Scooby-Doo, who would anchor two networks; create the teenage mystery genre; spin off different series; and conquer syndicated and cable television. CBS Programming Chief Fred Silverman started spinning off characters from hit shows, and the first dedicated animated television movie of the week was created. Strong African American characters and leading super female characters got their day in the spotlight as well.

Competitive Saturday morning television was well on its way to becoming a respected, revenue-generating division of the broadcast networks.

# ONE

# THE ANIMATION ACTION HERO

The animation action hero genre (1966–1968) was an absolute explosion of superhero programming that debuted in 1966 and created the first modern programming trend on Saturday morning. *Superman* became the first legitimate hit of the genre, and the *Batman/Superman Hour* became the last green-lit traditional superhero show of the 1960s. By the 1969–1970 season, *Superman* was still on the air, which made the series the longest-running superhero series of the 1960s. Listed on the next page are the shows that were a part of the animation action-hero genre.

| Series | Studio | Network | Year |
|--------|--------|---------|------|
| *The New Adventures of Superman* | Filmation Associates | CBS | 1966 |
| *The Marvel Super Heroes* | Grantray-Lawrence | Syndicated | 1966 |
| *Space Ghost/Dino Boy* | Hanna-Barbera | CBS | 1966 |
| *The Mighty Heroes* | Terrytoons | CBS | 1966 |
| *The Space Kidettes* | Hanna-Barbera | NBC | 1966 |
| *Frankenstein Jr. and the Impossibles* | Hanna-Barbera | CBS | 1966 |
| *The Super 6* | DePatie-Freleng | NBC | 1966 |
| *The Superman/Aquaman Hour of Adventure* | Filmation Associates | CBS | 1967 |
| *Spider-Man* | Grantray-Lawrence | ABC | 1967 |
| *The Fantastic Four* | Hanna-Barbera | ABC | 1967 |
| *Birdman and the Galaxy Trio* | Hanna-Barbera | NBC | 1967 |
| *Super President* | DePatie-Freleng | NBC | 1967 |
| *The Herculoids* | Hanna-Barbera | CBS | 1967 |
| *Shazzan* | Hanna-Barbera | CBS | 1967 |
| *Moby Dick and the Mighty Mightor* | Hanna-Barbera | CBS | 1967 |
| *Young Samson and Goliath* | Hanna-Barbera | NBC | 1967 |
| *The Banana Splits Adventure Hour (featuring the Arabian Knights and the Three Musketeers)* | Hanna-Barbera | NBC | 1968 |
| *The Batman/ Superman Hour* | Filmation Associates | CBS | 1968 |

# TBSOOL Episode #4, June 1992

There is no doubt that comic books have always served as the literary garden for studios who want to take a well-known character, or series, and adapt the subject for the small screen.

In 1966, Filmation Associates's animated adaptation of *Superman* proved to be a ratings winner and led to super spin-offs, which included *The Superman/Aquaman Hour of Adventure* (1967) and *The Batman/Superman Hour* (1968). During the 1973–1974 season, Hanna-Barbera created a vehicle for Batman and Robin, Superman, Aquaman, and Wonder Woman titled *The Super Friends. The Super Friends* was a watered-down adaptation of *The Justice League of America* comic book series. Nevertheless, for the first time ever, Superman, Aquaman, Wonder Woman, and Batman and Robin appeared together on the small screen. In the earlier animated versions, Superman had been paired with Aquaman and Batman, but in title only. Wonder Woman's animated appearance with the other Justice Leaguers was historical, but her membership with *The Super Friends* clashed directly with *The Justice League of America*'s comic book continuity. Wonder Woman resigned from the League in 1969 when she renounced her powers. She wasn't reinstated until 1976, almost three years after *The Super Friends* story line was established.

Wonder Woman's absence from *The Justice League of America* comic and her subsequent appearance on *The Super Friends* illustrates perfectly how comic book story lines often differ from their television counterparts. Because the adaptation is based on an original idea, the director, producer, writer, or television network has almost free rein in creating new scenarios for the characters. In most instances, the publisher works directly with the studio to ensure creditability. Bob Haney, who was a writer for DC Comics, wrote one of the first *Batman* scripts for Filmation Associates. Bob was also instrumental in creating the original *Teen Titans*, which was later adapted by Filmation in 1967. Former DC writer and artist Alex Toth was hired by Hanna-Barbera to keep *The Super Friends* on track.

Over in the Marvel universe, the Hulk, Thor, Captain America, the Sub-Mariner, and Iron Man appeared in limited animated adventures titled *The Marvel Super Heroes* (1966). The musical themes were great ("Tony Stark, makes you feel, he's a cool exec with a heart a steel"). In 1967, Hanna-Barbera's adaptation of Marvel's *Fantastic Four* told the story of four ordinary folks who were mutated into superpowered beings after returning from a mission in space. Reed Richards became the stretchable Mr. Fantastic; his wife Sue became the Invisible Girl; Sue's brother, impetuous Johnny Storm, became the Human Torch; and Reed's close friend Ben Grimm was molded into the unstoppable Thing ("It's clobberin' time"). The characterizations and scripts were sharp. The guest stars were phenomenal, including the Watcher, Galactus, and the Silver Surfer. To complete the Fantastic Four's "mood," Hanna-Barbera's musical director Ted Nichols delivered New York beatnik–inspired background musical tracks that complemented the Fantastic Four's atmosphere perfectly.

Also in 1967, Grantray-Lawrence's *Spider-Man* was being fully realized. *Spider-Man's* adaptation was right on target with personality, art, and villains that were being synergized by Ray Ellis' upbeat jazz backgrounds. During the second season, legendary animator and director Ralph Bakshi took over the production. Ralph Bakshi's influence and interpretation of Spidey was powerfully evident. Gone were *Spider-Man's* hordes of villains, which included the Vulture, the Green Goblin, and Dr. Octopus. In their place were psychotic villains, aliens, and power-mad scientists. (One crazy villain ripped Manhattan from its roots and held the island for ransom.) I believe Bakshi wanted viewers to understand the psychology behind Spider-Man's character by directing concise, mature, and sometimes deadly stories. How Bakshi managed to make all these creative changes right under the network censors' noses is a miracle in itself.

## COMMENTARY ON CHAPTER 1: THE ANIMATION ACTION HERO

When I was a kid, I didn't watch *The Marvel Super Heroes* or *Spider-Man* on a regular basis. However, when both series went into syndication, I became an instant fan. By the 1968–1969 season, the superhero backlash was in full effect. With the Vietnam War going on at the same time, publications such as *The Christian Science Monitor* were concerned that there was too much violence on Saturday morning television. Also during the 1968–1969 season, *The Archie Show* debuted, and as the ratings for *The Archie Show* started to outpace the superhero shows, the networks changed their programming strategies, which gave birth to the Music Renaissance.

# Two

# THE MUSIC RENAISSANCE

In 1968, with the coverage of the Vietnam War being aired on the six o'clock news, network executives decided the time had come to curb the violence presented on Saturday morning television. In one sweeping moment, action and adventure was out, and teenage rock bands were in.

## TBSOOL EPISODE #3, MAY 1992

The successful comic-to-cartoon adaptation of the *Archie* comic book series created an entire new genre in children's television titled the Music Renaissance. The Music Renaissance era, which took place from 1968 to 1978, was one of the most creative and competitive periods for the Big 5 studios (Hanna-Barbera, Filmation Associates, Sid and Marty Krofft Productions, Rankin-Bass, and DFE). One of the best programs to emerge from the Music Renaissance was *Josie and the Pussycats*. Created by Dan DeCarlo in 1963, *Josie* comics generated good sales. Both Archie and Josie comic magazines shared the same publishing home, artists, and writers.

While it was evident that Hanna-Barbera was the number-one studio, their royal reign was about to be seized by Filmation's Music Renaissance king, *The Archies*. Undaunted, Hanna-Barbera launched *Josie and the Pussycats* as their main contender for the Music Renaissance crown. *Josie's* unprecedented television contract stipulated that CBS would order sixteen episodes. In addition, the cast of *Josie and the Pussycats* would host educational wraparounds titled *In the Know*.

Ted Nichols, Hanna-Barbera's musical director, was instrumental in making *Josie and the Pussycats* one of the biggest hits of the Music Renaissance. Ted composed some new musical background tracks for the comedy portions of *Josie*. For the adventure portions, Ted selected some of his best background musical tracks from *Jonny Quest, The Fantastic Four,* and *The Arabian Knights*, which created the right mood for Josie's dangerous encounters with villains and terrorists. Three singer-musicians were hired to play the Pussycats: Patrice Holloway, Cathy Dougher, and Cherie Moor. These singers blended their voices perfectly to create soulful harmonies.

To meet the demands of so many musical plots and story lines, many studios hired up-and-coming musical bands to work with their veteran musical composers, such as Ray Ellis (Filmation), Maury Laws (Rankin-Bass), and Hoyt Curtin (Hanna-Barbera).

Singer Michael Gray was hired to supply the singing voice for *Fat Albert and the Cosby Kids*. La-La Productions used their musical talent to shape the funk, rock, and blues sounds of *Josie and the Pussycats*. Producer Don Kirshner and singer Ron Dante provided the musical vocals for *The Archies*'s famous bubblegum pop. Ray Ellis' easy listening and pop tunes were just the right mix of background music for the *Brady Kids* series. The Hardy Boys Band provided the new *Hardy Boys* cartoon with real rock music and a funky dancer named Wanda Kay. The famous Jackson 5 provided their audiences with the right mix of Motown, which set off a master mix dance party. The rock sounds of Kaptain Kool and the Kongs were funky and fresh enough for the band to host *The Krofft Supershow*. *Kidd Video*, which arrived on the airwaves long after the post–Vietnam War era, was the first musical comedy program to showcase the real band members in live-action videos, as well as their cartoon counterparts on the same program.

My favorite all-around composer during this exciting era was Hoyt Curtin, who wrote great background music for *The Flintstones, The Jetsons,* and *Top Cat*. Hoyt was a magnificent songwriter and composer whose musical style was classic and flawless. Directors, producers, artists, writers, and animators are very important to the production of a cartoon series, but it is the man or woman behind the music that is responsible for getting an emotional response from viewers by setting the right mood and providing the musical personality of the series.

Cable television has not come to the hood (Brooklyn, New York); however, I managed to view *The Ren & Stimpy Show*, which airs on Nickelodeon. I think anyone who has seen this cartoon from hell would agree that the animation, scripts, and characterizations are superior, and the background music, edited by Bill Griggs and Brian Mars, features a classic assortment of different musical styles.

In a story titled "Fire Dogs," our heroes walk into town, starved and hungry. The musical style used for that scene is reminiscent of Carl Stalling's musical scoring of the *Looney Tunes* cartoons. Later, when Ren and Stimpy rescue a woman as fire dogs, the tempo of the background music picks up big time. The scene is reminiscent of that great "chase me, chase me" background music that was used for *The Perils of Penelope Pitstop* (Ted Nichols, 1969). Finally, when Stimpy puts out the fire (and he didn't use water either, folks), the music slows down to a classic yet contemporary jazz beat that is reminiscent of Johnny Holiday's fine instrumental backgrounds during his work on Bob Kane's *Courageous Cat and Minute Mouse* in 1960.

*The Archies* were the leaders of the Music Renaissance. From left to right: Betty Cooper, Archie Andrews, Jughead Jones, Reggie Mantle, Veronica Lodge, and Hot Dog. *The Archies* used by permission. Copyright Archie Comics Publications, Inc.

## COMMENTARY ON CHAPTER 2:
## THE MUSIC RENAISSANCE

*The Archie Show* proved to be a game changer and helped the CBS network maintain their number-one status. The following television season (1969–1970), ABC and NBC took advantage of the new musical trend; studios as well as networks sought out talented musicians to give their animated and live-action shows musical voices that would hopefully translate into successful ratings. The wonderful Music Renaissance bands representing each network are listed on the next page.

| Series | Band Name | Studio | Network | Year |
|---|---|---|---|---|
| *The Archie Show* | The Archies | Filmation Associates | CBS | 1968 |
| *The Banana Splits Adventure Hour* | The Banana Splits | Hanna-Barbera | NBC | 1968 |
| *The Hardy Boys* | The Hardy Boys | Filmation Associates | ABC | 1969 |
| *The Cattanooga Cats* | The Cattanooga Cats | Hanna-Barbera | ABC | 1969 |
| *The Archie Comedy Hour* | The Archies | Filmation Associates | CBS | 1969 |
| *The Bugaloos* | The Bugaloos | Sid and Marty Krofft | NBC | 1970 |
| *Josie and the Pussycats* | Josie and the Pussycats | Hanna-Barbera | CBS | 1970 |
| *The Harlem Globetrotters* | The Harlem Globetrotters | Hanna-Barbera | CBS | 1970 |
| *Scooby-Doo, Where Are You!* | Scooby-Doo (season 2) (8 episodes) | Hanna-Barbera | CBS | 1970 |
| *Archie's Funhouse (featuring the Giant Jukebox)* | The Archies | Filmation Associates | CBS | 1970 |
| *Sabrina and the Groovie Goolies* | The Groovie Goolies | Filmation Associates | CBS | 1970 |
| *Lancelot Link, Secret Chimp* | The Evolution Revolution | Sandler-Burns-Marmer Productions | ABC | 1970 |
| *The Jackson 5* | The Jackson 5 | Rankin-Bass in association with Motown | ABC | 1971 |
| *The Pebbles and Bamm-Bamm Show* | Pebbles and her Unusuals (one episode) | Hanna-Barbera | CBS | 1971 |
| *Fat Albert and the Cosby Kids* | Fat Albert's Junk Yard Band | Filmation | CBS | 1972 |
| *The Osmonds* | The Osmonds | Rankin-Bass | ABC | 1972 |
| *The Amazing Chan and the Chan Clan* | The Chan Clan Band | Hanna-Barbera | CBS | 1972 |

| *The Brady Kids* | The Brady Kids | Filmation | ABC | 1972 |
|---|---|---|---|---|
| *Josie and the Pussycats in Outer Space* | Josie and the Pussycats | Hanna-Barbera | CBS | 1972 |
| *The Flintstone Comedy Hour* | The Bedrock Rockers | Hanna-Barbera | CBS | 1972 |
| *Kid Power* | Kid Power | Rankin-Bass | ABC | 1972 |
| *Mission Magic* | Rick Springfield | Filmation | ABC | 1973 |
| *Butch Cassidy and the Sundance Kids* | Butch Cassidy and the Sundance Kids | Hanna-Barbera | NBC | 1973 |
| *Partridge Family 2200 A.D.* | The Partridge Family | Hanna-Barbera | CBS | 1974 |
| *The Hudson Brothers Razzle Dazzle Show* | The Hudson Brothers | Blye-Bearde Productions | CBS | 1974 |
| *The U.S. of Archie* | The Archies | Filmation | CBS | 1974 |
| *The Krofft Supershow* | Kaptain Kool and the Kongs | Sid and Marty Krofft | ABC | 1976 |
| *Jabberjaw* | The Neptunes | Hanna-Barbera | ABC | 1976 |
| *The New Archie/Sabrina Hour* | The Archies | Filmation | NBC | 1977 |
| *The Krofft Superstar Hour* | Bay City Rollers | Sid and Marty Krofft | NBC | 1978 |

## More Information Regarding the Music Renaissance

*The Banana Splits* was the only series to appear on both the Animation Action and Music Renaissance charts, since the series featured both animated action and musical entertainment.

Don Kirshner was a renowned songwriter and record producer who, along with producer Jeff Barry, created the musical tone for *The Archies* as well as the unseen musical band who sang the soulful music during the Harlem Globetrotters' basketball games. In 1969, *The Archies'* hit song "Sugar Sugar" spent four weeks on the Billboard Charts as the number-one song.

Ray Ellis was a musical director and arranger who worked with such legendary artists as Billie Holiday and Lena Horne.

Danny Janssen was the principal producer and writer of the *Josie and the Pussycats* album and the second season music for Scooby-Doo, Where Are You!

*In the Know* were educational wraparounds hosted by the *Josie and the Pussycats* cast that aired as educational shorts between each CBS Saturday morning show during the 1970–1971 season. *In the Know* would transition into *In the News* during the 1971–1972 season, and finally, *In the News* would transition to *30 Minutes* with host Christopher Glenn, airing from 1978 to 1982.

Record producer Mike Curb wrote songs for *The Cattanooga Cats* and the animated *Hot Wheels* LP albums in 1969.

# THREE
# THE SATURDAY MORNING MOVIE

There have always been animated and live-action movies and specials for kids. However, during the 1972–1973 season, ABC and CBS created their own versions of the TV movie of the week that served as back-door pilots for potential new programming.

## TBSOOL EPISODE #2, APRIL 1992

*The ABC Saturday Superstar Movie* was the first ever animated movie of the week for Saturday morning television. The sixty-minute *Saturday Superstar Movie* featured the animated versions of *Lost in Space, Nanny and the Professor, Gidget, The Brady Bunch, Oliver Twist, Willie Mays and the Say Hey Kid* (the autobiography of Willie Mays), plus a new production of *Looney Tunes* featuring Daffy Duck and Porky Pig.

Not to be outdone, CBS created *The New Scooby-Doo Movies*. Scooby's program was expanded to an hour-long format and competed with *The Saturday Superstar Movie* by using well-known celebrity voices and featuring guest stars like Sonny and Cher, Phyllis Diller, Jonathan Winters, Don Knotts, the Addams Family, and the Three Stooges. During the second season, the battle of the animated movies heated up with both *Superstar* and *Scooby* being renewed with new movies.

I believe the purpose of these movies was to provide a variety of animated entertainment for the viewing audience (children didn't want to watch the live-action, critically acclaimed *CBS Children's Film*

*Festival)*, and these new animated movies helped fill the void. *The New Scooby-Doo Movies* spun off a few television series, but none for CBS. Batman and Robin, who made two guest appearances on *The New Scooby-Doo Movies*, were spun off into a program titled *The Super Friends* for ABC (1973–1974), and *The Addams Family* was sent to NBC to appear in a new animated series (1973–1974).

ABC had better luck with some of their *Saturday Superstar* movies. *Yogi's Ark Lark*, which featured almost every talking animal and insect to ever be featured in a Hanna-Barbera cartoon, was successfully spun off into a weekly Saturday morning series for the network, titled *Yogi's Gang* (1973–1974). *Lassie and the Spirit of Thunder Mountain* was a *Saturday Superstar Movie* that dealt with crooked developers trying to destroy Native American burial grounds. The following season, ABC repackaged Lassie (literally, not figuratively) into a series titled *Lassie's Rescue Rangers* (1973–1974).

I'm not really sure who won this battle of the animated movie; both programs premiered in September 1972, and both were canceled in September 1974. The old version of *Scooby-Doo* did return for two seasons (1974–1976) before Scooby jumped ship to ABC to star in a new vehicle titled *The Scooby-Doo/Dynomutt Hour*. Yikes!

## COMMENTARY ON CHAPTER 3: THE SATURDAY MORNING MOVIE

*The Scooby-Doo/Dynomutt Hour*
I wasn't a huge fan of *The Scooby-Doo/Dynomutt Hour*. First of all, the actress who played Velma (Nicole Jaffe) was replaced by actress Pat Stevens, and her voice didn't quite sound like Nicole Jaffe's Velma characterization. The theme song was also lackluster when compared to the original *Scooby-Doo* opening theme song from 1969. However, after reading Joe Barbera's book, *My Life In 'toons: From Flatbush to Bedrock in Under a Century*,[1] I found out that CBS refused to renew *Scooby-Doo* even though the series, which was out of production, continued

---

[1] Joe Barbera, *My Life In 'toons: From Flatbush to Bedrock in Under a Century* (Atlanta: Turner Publishing, Inc., 1994), 179–181.

to score high ratings. Scooby was eventually shopped to ABC and pitched to Vice President of Daytime and Children's Programming Michael Eisner. Without missing a beat, Michael Eisner green-lit the new *Scooby-Doo/Dynomutt Hour.*

*Scooby-Doo* still continues today and is the last great Hanna-Barbera creation to reach the coveted evergreen status, which places Scooby-Doo in a category with other iconic characters, such as Superman and Bugs Bunny, whose images and personalities continue to be successful with every new generation of audiences.

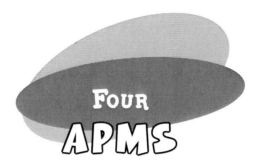

# FOUR
# APMS

As my television viewing habits became more sophisticated, I noticed that some of my favorite characters' designs would change without any explanation. I later found out that some of these changes happened when new studios took over the show or character. Nonetheless, I found the different looks fascinating and came to link the characters' changing facelifts with a particular studio or production.

## TBSOOL EPISODE #5, JULY 1992

In the not-too-distant past, legendary cartoon stars Bugs Bunny and Mickey Mouse celebrated fifty years in the business. Their respective studios (Warner Brothers and Disney) provided the media with plenty of old vintage footage and publicity stills, which showcased the veteran cartoon stars' APMs (artistic physical modifications). Automatically, I started thinking about all those other cartoon facelifts—APMs that take place in the industry but the public never hears about.

One such example is the noticeable differences between the Fleischer Brothers' version of Popeye's girlfriend, Olive Oyl, and the Famous Studios' repackaged version of Olive Oyl. Thick bangs were added to Olive's old hairstyle, giving the animated star an up-to-date coiffure. Secondly, to give Olive the illusion of beauty, circles were drawn around her dot eyes, and three to four eyelashes were added. After the makeup folks (artists) were through with her, Olive was sent to wardrobe for some final fittings. Her long trademark dress with the hem that went down to her flat feet during the 1930s was lifted to just below the knee. Finally, the studio threw in a pair of pumps, bringing Olive into what was then the modern era. This new, glamorous Olive Oyl finally gave credence to the infamous love triangle and aggressions between Popeye, Olive, and Bluto.

During the modern era of animation, many popular characters were modified from time to time. One such character was Penelope Pitstop, whose crazy antics could be seen every week on Hanna-Barbera's *Wacky Races* (1968). Penelope and another group of racers, the Ant Hill Mob, were spun off into a program titled *The Perils of Penelope Pitstop* (1969). Penelope was sent to makeup as well as to the APM plastic surgeon, who completely redesigned the character. Changes to Penelope included new eyes, a new coiffure, and a new wardrobe, plus the studio threw in a dashing new race car. The Ant Hill Mob, whose faces seemed nondescript and whose members had few speaking roles on *The Wacky Races* (because Dick Dastardly and Muttley stole every scene), were given new faces, names, and personalities. In all, seven Ant Hill Mob characters received redesigns, and thanks to the vocal talents of Janet Waldo, Paul Lynde, Don Messick, Paul Winchell, and Mel Blanc, *The Perils of Penelope Pitstop* featuring the Ant Hill Mob was a hit.

The new Penelope Pitstop makes her dramatic debut in *The Perils of Penelope Pitstop*. Licensed by: Warner Bros. Entertainment Inc. All Rights Reserved.

Other APMs followed. When a dog was needed for *The Brady Bunch* animated vehicle, Mop Top was created. Mop Top's design and body type were based on Hot Dog, who was the mascot for *The Archies*. The canine's size, features, and colors were modified to suit *The Brady Kids*, and the creation of Mop Top was complete. Mop Top joined Ping and Pong (two pandas) and Marlon, the mynah bird whose magical powers and smart mouth often brought the *Brady Kids* plenty of headaches.

APMs were represented in other subtle forms. The first set of *The Flintstones* designs from season one looked unsophisticated. The next set of designs that followed was of better quality, in my opinion; these episodes included "The Great Gazoo" era (featuring the voice of Harvey Korman). By the time *The Flintstones* graduated to the big screen in the theatrical release of *The Man Called Flintstone*, the animation and artwork were impressive.

## COMMENTARY ON CHAPTER 4: APMS

*Meeting Iwao Takamoto*
During a tour arranged by my Cartoon Network colleague Charles Lundsberg, I had the pleasure of meeting the great Iwao Takamoto at Warner Brothers Studios back in 2005. Iwao was the character and production designer, as well as producer of many Hanna-Barbera productions. I used the opportunity to ask him about Penelope Pitstop's redesign that he created for *The Perils of Penelope Pitstop*, and he told me that he wanted Penelope to look similar to the heroine from *The Perils of Pauline*. He also said Penelope was not supposed to be included in the original *Wacky Races TV Show*, but there was a pending toy deal, and the toy manufacturer wanted a girl racer. On the fly, Iwao created Penelope Pitstop so that Joe Barbera could present the new female character as part of the *Wacky Races* presentation to the toy manufacturer. Iwao also mentioned that Muttley's design (from *Wacky Races*) was based on the shape of a vacuum cleaner. While we were visiting with Iwao, he drew a picture of Scooby-Doo that now resides in the Cartoon Network programming department in Atlanta, Georgia.

*More about Olive Oyl*

What I didn't know in 1992 but found out later was that Paramount Studios actually took over Fleischer Studios in what could be described as a hostile takeover. The Fleischer Studios was changed to Famous Studios. The Popeye, Bluto, and Swee'Pea character designs were all modified to fit Famous Studios' house style, with Olive Oyl getting a complete makeover. In the Fleischer version, Olive's loyalty to Popeye was unwavering, but in the Famous Studios version, Olive developed a wandering eye and could be easily influenced by Bluto's physical attributes and flashy smile.

## My Final Word on The Flintstones

When I watched *The Flintstones* as a kid, I never noticed the differences in character design for the cast. However, later in life, I did notice, and while I believe the earlier seasons are better animated, I prefer the later character designs. I believe much of *The Flintstones* character design changed as Hanna-Barbera crafted and modified their house style. *Yogi Bear* also went through similar developmental character phases.

# FIVE

# ANIMATED AFRICAN AMERICANS AND SUPER TEENAGE DIVAS

Television programming in the 1960s was dominated by superheroes and later musical groups. However, by the 1969-1970 season, animated African Americans and super teenage divas were breaking barriers in a sea of traditional programming. Animated African Americans and super teenage divas stuck around and thrived through the next two decades.

## TBSOOL EPISODE #6, AUGUST 1992 (PART 1)

Hadji, the young East Indian orphan who shared his adventures on the *Jonny Quest* series, and Guru, the spiritual East Indian mystic who aided the government-based Cold War team from the animated version of *Fantastic Voyage*, were the only people of color during the early days of Saturday morning programming. African Americans and female headliners were nonexistent.

Historically, the first African American appearance took place on Filmation's animated version of *The Hardy Boys* (ABC, 1969). Pete Jones was voiced by actor Byron Kane and was one of the members of *The Hardy Boys'* musical band and the first African American to be presented as a positive image and role model on Saturday morning.

The lack of diversity was used to one television network's advantage when animated African Americans and super teenage divas were added to the CBS 1970–1971 Saturday morning schedule. In the prime 10:00 a.m.

time slot was Dan DeCarlo's *Josie and the Pussycats*, which was adapted from the comic pages of Archie Publications. *Josie* followed the misadventures of a female musical band called (what else) Josie and the Pussycats. Cast members included Josie, the band's leader; Melody, a hot platinum blonde and comic relief; Valerie, an African American superbrain; Alan, Josie's love interest; and Alexander Cabot, the Pussycats' manager and Josie's love interest (only in the comic book pages). The Alex-Josie romance was dropped when Josie was adapted for television. Rounding out the cast was Alexander's sister, Alexandra Cabot, the bitchiest scene-stealing, back-stabbing, and scheming animated female to ever come out of the inkwell at Hanna-Barbera Productions.

When plans were made to adapt *Josie* for television, story editors Joe Ruby and Ken Spears had no intention of duplicating the silly teenage fluff that made Josie so popular among comic readers. Instead, Ruby and Spears cleverly used all the in-fighting, gags, and hidden agendas of the characters to springboard *Josie and the Pussycats* into a world of adventure, comedy, and intrigue. Josie was the super teenage diva who kicked butt, captured terrorists, and played gigs. Helping Josie discombobulate the villains was Valerie. It was Valerie who always managed to get the Pussycats out of those deadly traps with her MacGyver-type know-how. It was Valerie who questioned the creditability of the situations that confronted the group. As the coolest Pussycat, Val was also the first animated African American female to be featured on a Saturday morning animated series.

In addition to the three actresses hired to play Josie, Valerie, and Melody, three musicians were hired to perform and sing as band members. Patrice Holloway, who played Valerie (from the musical side), was an African American singer who sang the opening theme song for the series. Patrice also alternated lead vocals with Cathy Dougher and Cherie Moor (a.k.a Cheryl Ladd—the former Charlie's Angel).

During the same championship television season, the world-famous Harlem Globetrotters made their first animated debut. A typical *Globetrotter* story line usually involved the basketball magicians being manipulated into a situation that required the team to play a game of basketball. The *Globetrotters* cast included Meadowlark Lemon, voiced by the late and talented Scatman Crothers; pessimist Freddie "Curly" Neal (Stu Gilliam); and forgetful Bobby Joe (Eddie "Rochester"

Anderson). Rounding out the cast were Gip (Richard Elkins); Gesse (Johnny Williams); Pabs (Robert DoQui); Granny, the Globetrotters' manager (Nancy Wible); and the team mascot, a dog named Dribbles. During the second half of any Globetrotter basketball game, R&B rhythm beats accompanied by soulful vocals enhanced the super athletic versatility of the Globetrotters as they played to victory.

## TBSOOL Episode #7, September 1992 (Part 2)

Sabrina the teenage witch, who made her debut in the *Archie Comedy Hour* (1969–1970 season), graduated to her own show during the 1970–1971 season: *Sabrina and the Groovie Goolies*. The Goolies lived on the outskirts of an unassuming all-American town named Riverdale. Riverdale, if you recall, is the home where America's most famous and oldest teenager, Archie Andrews, resides. Archie had no idea that his good friend Sabrina, super teenage diva, and all her relatives were witches, vampires, and werewolves. This paradox made *Sabrina and the Groovie Goolies* the hit of the 1970–1971 television season. When the Goolies weren't fussin' and zapping each other, these funky relatives of Sabrina were usually jamming with R&B and bubblegum pop harmonies. The Goolies were popular and the perfect supporting cast for Sabrina.

In 1971, with Diana Ross' likeness in the pivotal episode, *The Jackson 5*'s story was told animation-style. *The Jackson 5* featured little Michael Jackson, along with his brothers Jackie, Tito, Jermaine, and Marlon. Produced by Jules Bass and Arthur Rankin Jr., the show's stories related to the talented Jackson family's ability to help, encourage, and befriend folks from all walks of life. Of course, the best part of the show was *The Jackson 5*'s musical animated videos that featured such early hits as "Mama's Pearl" and "Never Can Say Good-bye." *The Jackson 5* was awarded an Action for Children's Television commendation.

In 1972, *Fat Albert and the Cosby Kids* settled in for several successful seasons on CBS. Hosted by the incomparable Bill Cosby, the cast included little Bill Cosby; his brother, Russell; Rudy; Weird Harold; Bucky; Dumb Donald; and Mush Mouth. *The Cosby Kids*' episodes focused on family values, morals, drug abuse, interracial marriages, fair play, and race relations. Bill Cosby won an Emmy Award for Outstanding Individual

Achievement in Children's Programming for *Fat Albert and the Cosby Kids* in 1981, and the show is considered a classic landmark television series.

The year 1972 also brought forward the first multicultural cartoon, *Kid Power*. Adapted from *Wee Pals*, the syndicated comic strip by Morrie Turner, *Kid Power* showcased a cast of young people from different ethnic backgrounds who were members of the Rainbow Club. The club's agenda: to preserve the Earth's environment and fight racial prejudice. With good scripts and great songs, the program left its viewers with the positive impression that the world can be a better place culturally, racially, and environmentally.

*I Am the Greatest: The Adventures of Muhammad Ali* (1977, NBC) was probably the only dud in the African American cartoon genre. With the help of producer Fred Calvert, Muhammad Ali—the legendary boxing champion—went down for the count. Muhammad's opponent: a shoestring budget and a lousy script. Part of the blame goes to NBC, whose programming standards were represented in this order: close-ups first, background music second, and animation dead last!

The animated version of *Mr. T* (1983) finally broke new ground on the same network. Mr. T was the first African American action hero to headline his own animated television series. The Ruby-Spears Production showcased the former bodyguard as the captain and coach of a gymnastics team that toured the country. Each week, the team encountered all sorts of trouble that required Mr. T to kick some butt and retort, "I pity the fool." At the end of each adventure, Mr. T appeared live to talk to viewers about the moral of the story.

There were more animated shows featuring African American characters. This list was originally printed in TBSOOL episode #22, February 1994.

## CHUCK CLAYTON AND HARRIET TUBMAN—DEBUT ON THE U.S. OF ARCHIE, 1974, CBS NETWORK

*The U.S. of Archie* was a weekly series that celebrated America's history and famous historical figures. While the Archie gang's descendants assisted such inventors as Robert Fulton and Alexander Graham Bell, cast member Chuck Clayton told viewers about his descendant, who was a conductor on Harriet Tubman's Underground Railroad. Chuck Clayton was the first African American character to become a regular in the *Archie* comic book and was the only African American character to make a celluloid appearance with Filmation's *Archie* series.

## Astraea of the Young Sentinels— Debut 1977, NBC Network

An alien, Sentinel One, endows three teenagers with super powers and eternal youth. Their mission: to preserve the Earth's environment and protect society (the usual stuff). These young sentinels included Hercules, Mercury, and Astraea, the first shape-shifting animated African American heroine. Astraea had the ability to transform her body molecules into any animal form. During the midseason, the title was changed to *The Space Sentinels* (which did nothing for the series' ratings).

## Superstretch and Microwoman— Debut 1978, CBS Network

*Superstretch and Microwoman* was an adventure segment that appeared on Filmation's powerhouse animated and live-action series *Tarzan and The Super Seven*. The twosome was the first animated African American married couple with super powers. Stretch, of course, possessed super elasticity, while Microwoman could shrink her body down to any size she desired. The couple resided in Southern California.

The following is a list of Saturday morning television and syndicated animated programs that continued the tradition of animated African Americans and super teenage divas during the 1980s and 1990s.

- DIC Enterprises
  - *Maxie's World (1987)*
  - *Beverly Hills Teens (1987)*
  - *The New Archies (1987)*
  - *C.O.P.S. (1988)*

- *The Karate Kid (coproduced with Saban Entertainment and Columbia Pictures Television, 1989)*
- *Camp Candy (coproduced with Saban Productions, 1989)*
- *Captain Planet (coproduced with TBS Productions, Inc., 1990)*
- *Hammerman (coproduced with Bustin' Productions, Inc., 1991)*
- *ProStars (coproduced with the Cookie Jar Company, 1991)*

- Ruby-Spears Enterprises
  - *Rickety Rocket (1979)—the first futuristic African Americans in space.*
  - *Mr. T (1983)—Marty Pasko, who helped shape Mr. T's solid story line, would use his storytelling skills as a story editor on Batman: The Animated Series.*
  - *Punky Brewster (1985)*

- Marvel Productions/TSR/Dungeons & Dragons Entertainment
  - *Dungeons & Dragons (1983)*

- Marvel Productions/Motown Productions/Saban Productions
  - *Kid 'n Play (1990)—the first rap stars to headline their own animated Saturday morning series.*

- Marvel Productions/Sunbow Productions/Hasbro Productions
  - *Jem (1985)—the first television series since Josie and the Pussycats to feature the misadventures of an all-girl band.*
  - *G. I. Joe: A Real American Hero (1985)*

- Murakami, Wolf, and Swenson, Inc./Will Vinton Productions
  - *The California Raisin Show (1989)*

- Murakami, Wolf, and Swenson, Inc./United Artists/Metro Goldwyn/Mayer Animation/Danjaq/RLR Associates
  - *James Bond Jr. (1991)*

- Hanna-Barbera Productions
  - *The Flintstone Kids (1986)—the first version of the Flintstones series to feature an African American character (Philo Quartz).*

- Sid and Marty Krofft Productions
  - *Pryor's Place (1984)—hosted by comedian Richard Pryor. After the show was praised by critics and viewers alike, CBS promptly canceled Pryor's Place, which resulted in scrutiny of the network.*

## COMMENTARY ON CHAPTER 5: ANIMATED AFRICAN AMERICANS AND SUPER TEENAGE DIVAS

Wow! My comments regarding the Muhammad Ali animated series and animated productions sold to NBC were harsh! NBC's fortunes would turn around thanks to programming chief Phyllis Tucker-Vinson during the 1981–1982 season with the introduction of *The Smurfs* series. *The Smurfs* was created by Belgian cartoonist Peyo (a.k.a. Pierre Culliford) and adapted by Hanna-Barbera for American audiences during the 1981–1982 season. *The Smurfs* would break NBC's perpetual third-place standing to become the first fantasy-adventure series to create the big bang phenomenon for NBC's Saturday morning schedule. The influence of *The Smurfs* was evident, as cutesy animated characters became the new programming trend, which included *The Shirt Tales* (1982, NBC), *The Monchhichis* (1983, ABC), *The Biskitts* (1983, CBS), *The Snorks* (1984, NBC), *The Paw Paws* (1985, syndicated), and *The Pound Puppies (*1986, ABC*).*

Also during the 1980s, Filmation Studios created the big bang phenomenon in the syndicated market by introducing first-run action-adventure programming with the launch of *He-Man and the Masters of the Universe* (1983). Additional syndicated hit series from this era included, *The Transformers* (1984), *ThunderCats* (1985), and *G.I.Joe—A Real American Hero* (1985). Additional action shows would soon follow the first-run-syndication programming trend.

# Six

# COMICS— THE DEATH OF SUPERMAN

*The Death of Superman* was a successful comic book tent-pole event that catapulted huge sales for DC Comics back in 1992. When I bought my issue that featured the death of the greatest hero of them all, CNN was at my comic book store, covering the historic event for posterity. Listed below is the original newsletter that discusses the big event and highlights Superman's animated television career.

## TBSOOL Episode #8, October 1992

Unless you've been living under a rock, the greatest hero of them all— Superman—kicked the bucket after fighting a superpowered villain named Doomsday. Sales of this historic battle have gone through the roof. In addition, customers (like myself) who were lucky enough to buy the special edition of this historic Superman story received an official black mourning armband, a Superman funeral procession poster (a real heartbreaker), Superman commemorative stamps, a *Daily Planet* obituary, and finally, one Superman-Doomsday trading card. My column has mentioned Superman's contributions to Saturday morning television on many occasions, so in memory of Earth's greatest hero, the following is a list of Superman's animated television career and highlights.

# SUPERMAN
# (FLEISCHER STUDIOS/FAMOUS STUDIOS) —
# DEBUT 1941, FULLY ANIMATED THEATRICAL SHORTS

The Academy Award–nominated *Superman* became an instant classic and brought the animation art form to a new heights. While these animated shorts were not made for television specifically, the Superman shorts were later syndicated for television.

# THE NEW ADVENTURES OF SUPERMAN
# (DC COMICS/FILMATION ASSOCIATES) —
# DEBUT 1966, CBS NETWORK

These were the first made-for-TV adventures of Superman. The phenomenal success of this series sent the other animation studios scrambling to buy the rights to every superhero adaptation they could get their hands on. During one such raid, Grantray-Lawrence, and later Ralph Bakshi, acquired Marvel's *Spider-Man* (1967), and Hanna-Barbera walked away with Marvel's *Fantastic Four* (1967). With dollar signs ringing in every network executive's ears, *The New Adventures of Superman* gave birth to Saturday morning programming as we know it today. This series also included *The Adventures of Superboy* and *Krypto, the Superdog.*

# THE SUPERMAN-AQUAMAN HOUR OF ADVENTURE
# (DC COMICS/FILMATION ASSOCIATES) —
# DEBUT 1967, CBS NETWORK

This super hour featured a powerhouse cast of DC Publications' top superheroes. Included were the solo adventures of Superman, Aquaman and Aqualad, Green Lantern, the Flash and Kid Flash, Hawkman, and the Atom. Also included were the adventures of the Justice League of America (Superman, the Flash, the Atom, Hawkman, and Green Lantern) and the Teen Titans (Speedy, Wonder Girl, Aqualad, and Kid Flash).

## THE BATMAN/SUPERMAN HOUR (DUCOVNY PRODUCTIONS INC. PRESENTATION — PRODUCED AT FILMATION ASSOCIATES) — DEBUT 1968, CBS NETWORK

This is the first animated *Batman* series that featured Robin, Batgirl, Alfred, Commissioner Gordon, and all the prominent Batman villains. Filmation produced a follow-up *Batman* series in 1977, which featured Bat-Mite. Superman's last Filmation appearance took place on *The Brady Kids* (September 1972, ABC Network).

## THE SUPER FRIENDS (HANNA-BARBERA STUDIOS) — DEBUT 1973, ABC NETWORK

*The Super Friends* debuted with watered-down adventures of *The Justice League of America*, featuring Superman, Batman and Robin, Aquaman, and Wonder Woman. This was also the first time all five heroes appeared together on the animated screen. Green Arrow, the Flash, and Plastic Man made guest appearances during the first season.

## THE ALL NEW SUPER FRIENDS HOUR (HANNA-BARBERA STUDIOS) — DEBUT 1977, ABC NETWORK

Hanna-Barbera created some new superheroes to fight alongside the Super Friends. Joining the cast was Black Vulcan, an African American hero whose main power was electricity. Apache Chief, a Native American hero who grew into a giant, and Rima the Jungle Girl, who had a short-lived comic series with DC Comics, rounded out the cast.

## CHALLENGE OF THE SUPERFRIENDS (HANNA-BARBERA STUDIOS) — DEBUT 1978, ABC NETWORK

This was the best-written *SuperFriends* series (also note, the title changed to one word).[2] Every week, Lex Luthor and his band of villains tried to conquer the world. In one episode, the villains destroyed the world, and Superman was Earth's sole survivor.

## SUPERMAN (RUBY-SPEARS PRODUCTIONS) — DEBUT 1988, CBS NETWORK

After a universal cataclysm ("Crisis on Infinite Earths") takes place, Superman's previous history and existence are replaced by a completely new reality. These post-Crisis animated Superman stories were a reflection of DC Comics' "Crisis on Infinite Earths" story line (1985). Also featured on the series was the *Superman Family Album*, which showcased Superman's early years as a child and teenager.

## COMMENTARY ON CHAPTER 6: COMICS — THE DEATH OF SUPERMAN

## ALLEN DUCOVNY AND GEORGE KASHDAN — DC COMICS' UNSUNG HEROES

Contrary to popular belief, the trinity (*The New Adventures of Superman*, *The Superman/Aquaman Hour of Adventure*, and *The Batman/Superman Hour*) were all coproductions between Filmation Associates and National Periodical Publications (DC Comics' former moniker, now known as DC Entertainment). By the time the third series was created and conceived, the credits were changed to reflect the prominence of

---

[2] Marc Tyler Nobleman, "The year when the title switched from *Super Friends* to *Superfriends* was 1978," *Noblemania*, last modified July 29, 2011, accessed August 12, 2014, http://noblemania.blogspot.com/2011/07/super-70s-and-80s-super-friendsdarrell.html.

DC Comics (Ducovny Production Inc. Presentation was listed as the first end credit).

When I visited Lou Scheimer at his home in 2007, he told me that Allen Ducovny was put in charge of the animated series because he was the only one working at National who had "media experience." Allen was instrumental in creating the *Superman Radio Show* during the 1940s, and he hired the actors from the radio show, Bud Collyer and Joan Alexander, to play Superman/Clark Kent and Lois Lane, respectively, in the animated series. Ducovny was also involved in casting Olan Soule to play the voice of Batman for the creation of *The Batman/Superman Hour*.

Years later, Allen Ducovny was hired by CBS as director of programming and was active in development of Filmation's *Isis* series (part of the *Shazam!/Isis Hour*), as well as being involved in the casting of Joanna Pang, who played the supporting role of student Cindy Lee during the first season of *Isis* (1975). When DC Comics adapted *Isis* for a comic book series in 1976 and later during the 52 story line (2006), it was great to find out that the origins of the Isis character started with Allen Ducovny, a DC Comics guy.

George Kashdan was the editor of several top-selling DC comics, including *Aquaman*. As editor of the *Aquaman* comic book series and writer on *The Superman/Aquaman Hour of Adventure*, Kashdan ensured that Black Manta (Aquaman's arch nemesis) would make his first comic book and television appearances in the fall of 1967. George was also the editor for *The Brave and the Bold* and *The Teen Titans* comic book series, the latter being scripted by Kashdan for the television adaption, which appeared on *The Superman/Aquaman Hour of Adventure*.

Like Ducovny, Kashdan also had media experience, having worked on *The Mighty Hercules* series in 1963. I'm sure that between Ducovny and Kashdan, they helped transition and implement training for some of the comic book writing staff, who had to learn how to write scripts for television. During the *Superman/Aquaman Hour*, television writer Dennis Marks was hired to write scripts. Dennis Marks went on to have a long and great television career. Marks also scripted one of my favorite series, Marvel's *Dungeons & Dragons*, for CBS (1983–1985). I believe that if Allen Ducovny and George Kashdan had not been involved in these productions, the creative results would have been entirely different.

## MORE INFORMATION ABOUT THE SUPER FRIENDS

The cast for *The All New Super Friends Hour* wasn't exactly rounded out, as I indicated in my original newsletter. Missing from the original newsletter was Samurai (a superhero created especially for the series). Also missing from the original newsletter were the other DC heroes that included the Atom, Hawkman, Hawkgirl, the Flash, and Green Lantern. Perhaps the biggest omission was not listing the Wonder Twins (Zan and Jayna) and their pet monkey, Gleek, who served as the new teenage sidekicks. Unlike Wendy and Marvin, the sidekicks from season one of *The Super Friends*, the Wonder Twins had super powers and could shape-shift into water or ice and animals, respectively. While many people in the industry love to hate Scooby-Doo's nephew, Scrappy-Doo, I wasn't a fan of the Wonder Twins or Wendy and Marvin.

*Challenge of the SuperFriends* is still my all-time favorite *Super Friends* series, which is why I did not list the other *Super Friends* series that followed *Challenge of the SuperFriends* in the original highlighted section of Superman's television career.

Darrell McNeil (an animator, writer, and Filmation historian) wrote an article for *Back Issue* magazine in 2004 titled "The Greatest Stories Never Told: The Greatest Series Never Sold" and recalled the story of how the *Brady Kids'* Superman episode, "Cindy's Super Friend," and the Wonder Woman episode, "It's All Greek to Me," initiated the creation of *The Super Friends* series.[3] McNeil says those episodes "were the highest-rated ones of the *Brady Kids Show*, which prompted ABC to team Superman and Wonder Woman with former CBS Saturday stars Aquaman and Batman to form TV's *Justice League*, the *Super Friends*."

The return of the superheroes to Saturday morning came at a cost. The networks did not want a repeat of the violent animated superheroes from the not-so-distant 1960s era. Every superhero series that was sold to the networks after the debut of *The Super Friends* could not feature

---

[3] Darrell McNeil, "The Greatest Stories Never Told: The Greatest Series Never Sold," *Back Issue*, August 2004, 13.

any fist fights or big battles. Of course, this network stipulation hurt shows like *The Super Friends*. According to Iwao Takamoto, Hanna-Barbera's production designer and producer, who wrote about *The Super Friends* experience in his book, *Iwao Takamoto—My Life with a Thousand Characters*, the Hanna-Barbera studio received "irate letters" from the DC Comics' staff who were disappointed with *The Super Friends* series. Iwao said, "They wanted our heads!"[4]

The nonviolent superhero trend would continue throughout the 1980s, and syndicated (non-network shows) were not immune to the trend. While the syndicated *Battle of the Planets* (1978) broke all the rules, *He-Man and the Masters of the Universe* and *ThunderCats*, which were both syndicated in the 1980s, demonstrated restraint when it came to violence and action sequences. *Batman: The Animated Series* and *X-Men* series, which debuted during the 1992–1993 season on FOX, finally returned animated superheroes to their glory fighting days and are reminiscent of the animated superheroes from the 1960s, who were allowed to actually throw a punch. With the success of the *Batman: The Animated Series* and *X-Men* series, the push to remove the passive superhero from airwaves was starting to make an impact.

---

[4] Iwao Takamoto and Michael Mallory, foreword by Willie Ito, *Iwao Takamoto: My Life with a Thousand Characters* (Mississippi: University Press of Mississippi, 2009), 152.

# SEVEN
# AN INTERVIEW WITH ROBBY LONDON

It was Lou Scheimer who helped me secure the Robby London interview. I faxed a list of questions to Robby London to get the interview process started. Ironically, we did not cover any of the items listed on the original interview request.

## TBSOOL EPISODE #9, JANUARY 1993

The first time I saw DIC on the small screen was after I read the closing credits for the hit television show *Inspector Gadget*. Since then, DIC has taken their proper and rightful place in the industry as one of the most progressive, recognizable, and respected forces in the competitive world of animated television. I asked Robby London, senior vice president of creative affairs and executive producer for most of DIC's animated productions, if there was any formula behind DIC's success. Robby believes it is "DIC's ability to identify and target key properties." Indeed, *Heathcliff; Dennis the Menace; Beverly Hills Teens; The Real Ghostbusters; C.O.P.S.; Alf: The Animated Series; Captain N: The Game Master; Hey Vern, It's Ernest!; The New Archies;* and *Super Mario Brothers* are just a handful of television hits that reflect what Robby calls hot properties.

Currently airing on FOX's Saturday morning schedule is DIC's *Super Dave: Daredevil for Hire.* In a recent episode, Super Dave was hired to transport America's most dangerous villain, Snarl Vicious, across the country. Snarl's escape during extradition caused pandemonium, hysteria, and big laughs. This was no surprise to Robby, who said, "*Super Dave* is good cartoon entertainment." In fact, Robby is very proud of *Super Dave*, as well as another hot DIC property, *Captain Planet*. "The year that *Captain Planet* was being developed," said Robby, "there weren't any television programs in the mainstream media that were addressing the environmental issue." He enthusiastically added, "*Captain Planet* is the number-one syndicated animated program, consistently beating out the Disney afternoon." *Captain Planet* won an Environmental Media Award (1991) with a subsequent Environmental Media Award nomination in 1992. At the end of each *Captain Planet* episode, the good Captain and the Planeteers encourage viewers to do their share to preserve the Earth's environment, stressing, "The power is yours!"

Robby London started out in the business working as a story analyst at American International Pictures. From there, he became a program coordinator for the acclaimed *Michael Jackson* radio show. Hardworking and ambitious, Robby secured freelancing assignments with Hanna-Barbera Productions. "*The Harlem Globetrotters* was an early script assignment," he recalled. Robby mastered and refined his creative talents, which landed him a position as executive story editor at Filmation Productions. Robby was one of the key players at Filmation who wrote the pilot and subsequent scripts for one of Filmation's biggest television hits, *He-Man and the Masters of the Universe*. London recalled, "Before the first script was even written, Thomas Radecki, who represented a watch-dog group, was already reporting that He-Man is violent."

Robby related an anecdote concerning He-Man and violence. "I was instructed to rewrite a scene that involved He-Man causing a branch to break after he attempted to rescue an animal from a tree." The rewrite was initialized by the late Arthur Nadel, who London said "was my mentor. I remember Arthur telling me, 'He-Man would never cause a branch to break.'" So the scene was rewritten, keeping He-Man's ultimately good image in tow. "Our critics' claims notwithstanding, most people in the industry try to write scripts that are pro-social and nonimitative. We are not wild people without any social conscience," London concluded.

DIC has had many successful endeavors on both network television and in the competitive syndication market. "As a corporate strategy," Robby explained, "we wouldn't want to sacrifice either market. The networks offer more concentrated viewers, higher budgets, promotions, and better quality for their programs. In the syndication markets you have the advantage of producing more episodes and taking advantage of economy of scale (the more you produce, the better the price break)." But Robby emphasized that "the financing in syndication can be more complex."

I told Robby that one of my personal DIC favorites was *The Defenders of Dynatron City*, which was a special produced for FOX Television. The story involved a futuristic society living hand in hand with safe atomic power. On occasion, this atomic power produced superpowered mutants, giving birth to *The Defenders of Dynatron City*.

The Defenders included Monkey Kid (degenerated into part human), Ms. Megawatt (Whoopi Goldberg), Jet Headstrom, Buzz Saw Girl, Tool Box, and Radium Dog.

Bob Forward, whose work I became familiar with during his BraveStarr days at Filmation, wrote an entertaining and fluid *Defenders* script. London, who served as executive producer of *The Defenders*, agreed with me about the quality of the show, but he also said, "FOX has no plans to pick up the series. *The Defenders of Dynatron City* was a very expensive program to produce and a strain on a network budget." Nevertheless, producing expensive, high gloss, fully-animated television programming has paid off tremendously for DIC. *Madeline*, the classic children's book whose literary adaptations were made into lavish fully-animated specials for HBO and the Family Network, was later nominated for an Emmy (1989) and the prestigious Humanitas Prize (1991). The latter award is given to television programs that reflect the most humane and positive depictions of life. DIC's *Camp Candy* won the Humanitas Prize in 1991.

Robby London is a hands-on executive who works double time juggling the creative, production, and administrative responsibilities as an executive producer. In his role as senior vice president, Robby meets the needs of the television networks, clients, and various "rights holders." With such a busy schedule, I asked Robby London if he had time to watch the competition. Without hesitation, he said, "Not enough."

Robby and I did talk about the new *Batman: The Animated Series*, and on that topic he said, "I think the production values are terrific." DIC's impressive debut in the '80s prompted me to ask about the company's strategy for the '90s and beyond. "To remain cutting edge," was Robby's quick and optimistic retort. He also added, "To create more original properties. Hopefully the industry will become more predisposed to original properties," London concluded. I'm sure whatever upheavals take place in the world of animation, DIC Enterprises will be there, ready to triumph!

## COMMENTARY ON CHAPTER 7: AN INTERVIEW WITH ROBBY LONDON

I have to admit, the entire interview process was a challenge, but thankfully, Robby was very patient with me, and by the time I was ready to interview Norm Prescott of Filmation Productions, I was better prepared. I never spoke to Robby London again but enjoyed his articles in *Animation Magazine* as well as his commentary on the *He-Man and the Masters of the Universe* DVD collection. I was really impressed with DIC Enterprises and believed that those productions were a good representation of the type of programming that was being produced in the 1980s and 1990s. I also like the fact that DIC Enterprises capitalized on the emerging digital technology to help give their productions an edge over the competition. By the way, DIC Enterprises stands for Diffusion, Information et Communication.

# Eight
# LIVE-ACTION ADVENTURES

Sid and Marty's Krofft's foray into live-action television production was important because studios in Hollywood were not producing live-action children's television productions on a regular basis for Saturday morning. However, when Hanna-Barbera secured high-end costumes and puppets from Sid and Marty Krofft for *The Banana Splits Adventure Hour* (NBC, 1968–1969), the following season, Sid and Marty Krofft introduced *H. R. Pufnstuf*, which established Sid and Marty Krofft Productions as players in the Saturday morning game. The success of *H. R. Pufnstuf* enabled the Krofft brothers to become a consistent staple in children's television, specializing in quirky musical live-action fun!

## TBSOOL Episode #0404, April 1993

*H. R. Pufnstuf*, which premiered on NBC during the 1969–1970 season, combined puppetry, fantasy, fairy tale, and song. I always felt that *H. R. Pufnstuf* was supposed to be the jazzed-up male version of *The Wizard of Oz* (minus the rainbow and sentiment). In the place of Dorothy and Toto were Jimmy (skillfully played by actor Jack Wild) and Freddy, a pint-sized golden flute whose one-of-a-kind status attracted the eye of Miss Witchiepoo (Billie Hayes).

Knowing that Jimmy and Freddy were inseparable (Freddy was usually nestled in Jimmy's shirt pocket), Witchiepoo hatched a scheme to dispose of Jimmy and kidnap Freddy. She lured the unsuspecting pair to her siren-singing ship, whose sweet song echoed to Jimmy, "Come and play with me, Jimmy. Come and play with me, and I will take you on a trip far across the sea." Witchiepoo's kidnap attempt failed. Jimmy and Freddy washed up on Living Island, where they are befriended by the island's mayor, H. R. Pufnstuf, a large dragon with a Southern accent and a heart of gold.

In addition to the kidnapping attempts, Witchiepoo often thwarted Jimmy's plans to leave Living Island, which only made the youngster more aggressive, feisty, and resourceful. As a kid watching *H. R. Pufnstuf*, I often envisioned myself playing the lead role. After all, I was the right age and thought the part of Jimmy (the kid who gets kidnapped and transported to another dimension) was a great role. Unfortunately, I was never considered for the part! Nonetheless, I realized the selection of Jack Wild was impeccable.

While I appreciated the fact that Jimmy refused to play victim, I also looked forward to seeing what Witchiepoo was cooking up. Billie Hayes was the consummate scene stealer and wickedly delivered zinging insults to her incompetent aides (Orson Vulture and Stupid Bat). While Witchiepoo's machinations infuriated the kindhearted Pufnstuf, Witchiepoo definitely knew how to keep the atmosphere on the island crackling with excitement. Jimmy took up residence on Living Island for three years (NBC, 1969–1972) and then jumped ship to ABC for one season (1972–1973). How popular was *H. R. Pufnstuf*? Kids loved *Pufnstuf* so much that they watched the same seventeen episodes for years (because NBC was cheap, cheap, cheap)!

If *H. R. Pufnstuf* had been a prime-time series, there would have been at least one hundred episodes. Other Krofft productions of choice included *Lidsville*, the funky up-to-date male version of *Alice in Wonderland* (ABC, 1971–1973), and the psychedelic, upbeat *Bugaloos*, with comedienne Martha Raye (NBC, 1970–1972).

## COMMENTARY ON CHAPTER 8: LIVE-ACTION ADVENTURES

Sid and Marty Krofft Productions was on my original mailing list, and when they read the *H. R. Pufnstuf* newsletter, the Krofft brothers had

Joe King call me to find out how a guy living in Brooklyn, New York, knew so much about their series. Joe told me that I was one of the few people who got the episode count correct! Listed below is the letter from Joe King, sent on behalf of Sid and Marty Krofft Productions.

May 27, 1993

Mr. Mark McCray
Editor-in -Chief
TBSOOL
1203 Dean Street
Brooklyn, NY 11216


Dear Mark,

I really enjoyed our telephone conversation of yesterday, and once again I would like to express our appreciation for the recognition accorded to *H.R. Pufnstuf* in your most recent newsletter.

I have enclosed a copy of "Executive Suites" which you may find useful as reference material, as well as *H.R. Pufnstuf* T-shirts for you and Joy as a gift from Sid and Marty.

Many thanks again for your support.

Sincerely,

Joseph P. King
Executive Vice President


cc:   MKrofft
      SKrofft

SID & MARTY KROFFT PICTURES CORPORATION, 419 NORTH LARCHMONT BOULEVARD, SUITE 11, LOS ANGELES, CALIFORNIA 90004. 213-467-3125, FAX 213-932-6332

# NINE
# CLASSIC JAPANESE IMPORTS

Nowadays, all Japanese animation is described as anime, but back in 1993, I didn't know the word existed, which is why I created my own category for the genre—classic Japanese imports.

## TBSOOL EPISODE #0505, MAY 1993

Dr. Boynton to Astro Boy: "I'm going to be a good father to you too, my son. I'm going to teach you everything there is to know. I'll teach you how to fly, how to swim oceans, leap over mountains, how to be the bravest boy in the whole world. I'll be proud of you, son."

I was first introduced to *Astro Boy* by my father, Eugene McCray, who made sure our male-bonding television schedule consisted of *Astro Boy* at 11:00 a.m. and *Jeopardy* at 11:30 a.m. At noon, the school bus would come for my half day of kindergarten. My reintroduction to *Astro Boy* came through the local video store. After a close examination of such classic Japanese imports (CJIs) as *Astro Boy* and *Speed Racer*, I came to the realization that these CJIs were just as limited in animation style as their American counterparts. The true strength of these cartoons has always been, in short, great stories and characterizations.

The very first episode of *Astro Boy* is an emotionally heavy-handed story that tackles death, exploitation, slavery, power, greed, and love. Not even the most literal American cartoons of the 1960s dared touch such hot topics. While I found the pacing of the story slow, before I knew it, I was reeled in like a big fish! As each scene of *Astro Boy* is played out with emotion and passion, the viewer is shown the harsh realities of the real world. Created by Osamu Tezuka and adapted for American audiences by Fred Ladd in 1963, *Astro Boy*'s origin unfolds with a blue-plate special full of tragedy and drama. A car accident kills the son of Dr. Boynton, who is the head of the Institute of Science. The grieving doctor orders the other scientist to build a super robot in the likeness of his son. Boynton's colleagues follow his instructions but mumble to themselves that the doctor is going mad. The super robot is constructed within a year, and Boynton is pleased with the results. Instead of cigars and champagne wishes, the birth of Astro is culminated with the orchestration of Beethoven's Fifth Symphony, which is supplied by Boynton's synthesizer-computer-funk apparatus.

The synthesizer activates a main switch, which brings Astro Boy to life. This scene is quite eerie and is reminiscent of the classic horror film *Frankenstein*. Once Astro's power transfer is complete, the camera cuts to a close-up of Astro opening his eyes, which is followed by another close-up of Astro moving his robotic limbs for the first time. He stumbles as he attempts to walk. The camera cuts to an over-the-shoulder shot of Dr. Boynton watching his new son take his first steps. The father and son embrace. A tear flows from Dr. Boynton's eye, and the scene fades to black. Beautiful!

Physically, Astro Boy resembled a normal boy, but his face reminded me of Betty Boop, with his luminous eyes and Marlene Dietrich eyebrows. His boots could be described as long socks that converted into rockets for flight. He possessed super strength but wasn't omnipotent. Astro was also programmed with emotions and a moral code. Life was peachy keen until Boynton realizes that his new son wasn't physically growing. Instead of Boynton admitting that he made a mistake during the configuration and design of Astro, he lashes out in daddy-dearest melodrama and sells Astro Boy to an unscrupulous circus owner named Caccitore.

Astro Boy: "You sold me, you sold me. I can't believe it!"

Dr. Boynton: "You're not a human child. You're nothing but a machine, like a refrigerator or a dishwasher. Remember, you're a robot!"

Astro immediately becomes the big attraction of the robotic circus. That's when Dr. Packadermus J. Elefun, who has been appointed the new head honcho of the Institute of Science, enters Astro's troubled life. Outraged by the treatment of Astro Boy, Elefun tells Caccitore that Astro is a masterpiece of science and should be returned to the Institute of Science. Caccitore tells Elefun to take him to court.

A few days later, one hundred thousand robots protest the government, demanding and later winning their right to be free! As a free robot, Astro decides to stay with Dr. Packadermus J. Elefun, who becomes his mentor and friend. While most of Astro's adventures are action-packed, many stories depict him as a normal youngster, playing happily and being mischievous. He is, for all intents and purposes, a real boy!

## COMMENTARY ON CHAPTER 9: CLASSIC JAPANESE IMPORTS

Fred Ladd was the first commercial producer to introduce such anime classics as *Astro Boy* and *Gigantor* to American audiences. I had the pleasure of meeting Fred Ladd in 2004 when he paid a visit to the Cartoon Network programming team. We talked about *Astro Boy* and *Gigantor* as well as his colleague, former Filmation Productions cofounder Norm Prescott, who partnered with Fred Ladd to coproduce the theatrical movie *Pinocchio in Outer Space* (1965). *Gigantor* "the space age robot" (1964) was another huge anime success that Fred Ladd adapted for American audiences. Ladd's contribution to the competitive kids' industry created untapped opportunities for the kids' market, advertisers, and networks, and exposed audiences to new animated entertainment.

Fred autographed a *Gigantor* cast photo for me during his visit to Cartoon Network, which reads, "To Mark McCray: the all-knowing. Best wishes, Fred Ladd." The cast of *Gigantor*: Inspector Blooper, Dick Strong, Jimmy Sparks (holding the Gigantor controller), Dr. Bob Brilliant, and Gigantor.

Gigantor used by permission. Fred Ladd, Greatest Tales Company.

# TEN
# AN INTERVIEW WITH NORM PRESCOTT

## TBSOOL EPISODE #0406, JUNE 1993

Norm Prescott is a cool and down-to-earth kind of guy. While I knew and admired his work at Filmation Studios, I discovered that Norm had other successful careers long before the animation bug got in his system. A native of Boston and a natural talent in the broadcast booth, Norm rose to prominence in the late 1940s and early 1950s first in Boston and then in New York as WNEW's new personality. DJ Prescott delivered "rock 'n' roll and the big bands" to his radio audience for twelve years. "It was the single singer era and in-between eras," said Prescott, whose playlist of singing stars included Tony Bennett, Perry Como, and Frankie Laine.

In 1959, Joe E. Levine, who had just created Embassy Pictures, was looking for the right candidate to head the studio's music merchandising and postproduction division. Levine's impeccable choice was Prescott, who Levine named as vice president of music merchandising and postproduction. Hardly having the time to catch his breath, Norm's first project was to oversee the music supervision and postproduction for the Embassy Picture classic *Hercules*. In 1965, Prescott produced his first full-length animated feature, *Pinocchio in Outer Space*, for Universal Pictures.

Also in 1965, along with Lou Scheimer, Norm created Filmation Associates. "We were trying to develop an animation studio from scratch and were unable to break in," explained Prescott. "Hanna-Barbera was the number-one studio and had an unwritten credo of producing shows without partners. They would try to buy the property outright or create characters that were similar. In order for Filmation to make it, we became everyone's partners."

One of those first successful partnerships came with the adaptation of *The New Adventures of Superman* to the small screen in 1966. The success of *Superman* created the animation action hero genre (1966–1968), which opened the door for other studios to launch their superheroes and superheroines on Saturday morning television. When the animation action hero era was winding down, Filmation launched *The Archie Show*, which in turn created the Music Renaissance (1968–1978).

Over the years, Filmation quietly worked over the competition with innovative animated and live-action fare. Filmation was also responsible for implementing programming trends and standards that the rest of the industry adhered to. Norm Prescott heads up his own independent company these days; the company's achievements include the development of a cutting-edge process used for the colorization and restoration of black-and-white films.

When I caught up with Norm, he was busy "developing software for computer animation," which, he added, "is a challenge. You cannot do computer animation for the same cost as traditional animation." But, he says, "I'm working on getting the cost down." While it is evident that Norm has been in the business for more than forty years, I had the opportunity to talk to him about some of the great middle years of his career—the years Norm spent at Filmation.

TBSOOL:    Superman was a tremendous hit for Filmation. How did the project get initiated?

PRESCOTT: When I was working with Joe Levine on *Hercules,* I met with Mort Weisinger of DC Comics to discuss Superman and Hercules appearing in a story together. Mort said it was a great idea. "Let's do it." DC Comics sold Superman to CBS in 1965. Mort read the review for *Pinocchio in Outer Space* and remembered that I was the guy from Embassy. He called and said, "What are you guys up to?" and wanted to know if we were interested in producing *Superman*. I flew to New York and made the deal. I showed the network a sample of *Pinocchio in Outer Space*. Fred Silverman decided that *Superman* should be made into a series, which launched his career and gave Filmation immediate recognition as a producer in the industry.

TBSOOL:    I consider *Fantastic Voyage* Filmation's first adult television series. I always got the impression that there were Cold War overtones in the story line. Was Filmation going for the Cold War angle?

PRESCOTT:  No. We wanted to go into the microcosmic worlds that existed in a drop of rain water, a snowflake, a leaf, a rock, etc., where we could create all kinds of characters. The network was against the idea. So we never got to do it.

TBSOOL:    In one of my past newsletters, I mentioned that in one sweeping moment, action-adventure was out and music/comedies were in. The Vietnam War was one factor. Do you recall any other reasons for the changes in children's programming?

PRESCOTT:  There was a lot of pressure from parent groups, which were saying the networks were not looking out for kids. We decided to switch gears and create shows about real kids with real problems, and *Archie* was the obvious choice.

TBSOOL:    Was the musical angle for *The Archies* Filmation's idea?

PRESCOTT:  Absolutely. I knew the record world from my disc jockey days. We hired Don Kirshner to create *The Archies*. We got top writers and introduced bubblegum rock to Saturday morning television. At Hanna-Barbera, they played around with rock 'n' roll, but it was pseudo rock 'n' roll. "Sugar, Sugar" and "Bang-Shang-A-Lang" were two and a half million sellers. *The Groovie Goolies* song, "Chick-A-Boom" became a hit and later a commercial for Kentucky Fried Chicken.

TBSOOL:     *The Archies* broke all sorts of records in terms of television renewals, formats, etc. What was Filmation's formula for success?

PRESCOTT:   You have to understand, the normal buying pattern of the network was to buy thirteen shows and run them for two years. *The Archies* kept getting the numbers and did so well consistently that the network didn't want to let it go.

TBSOOL:     Were there any programs that you were particularly proud of?

PRESCOTT:   *Fat Albert and the Cosby Kids*. It was the first all-black animated program presented on national television. We hired Gordon Berry, who worked at the UCLA Educational Department as an advisor to help on the scripts. He worked with us, making sure the problems of each show were accurate and helped us communicate positive social values to young viewers. *Fat Albert* set a high standard. The television network hired Gordon away from us to go work for them! That was quite a compliment.

TBSOOL:     By the way, *Fat Albert and the Cosby Kids* received the best cartoon series nod in *TV Guide*'s fortieth anniversary issue.

PRESCOTT:   That's quite a kudo, isn't it? Out of all the shows from the 1970s, *TV Guide* felt that *Fat Albert and the Cosby Kids* was the best.

TBSOOL: *Uncle Croc's Block, Waldo Kitty,* and *Mission Magic* were very different animated/live-action programs from Filmation. Although these programs were not well received, the creative effort and originality were there. Any comments?

PRESCOTT: Things did not come out the way we wanted. It happens to all producers.

TBSOOL: How involved did you get in terms of selecting properties, character development, music, and scripts?

PRESCOTT: Lou and I operated as one person. We shared an office. We could tune in and tune out on each other's conversations. Lou worked closely with the writers, while I directed the talent, but most things we shared.

TBSOOL: *Journey Back to Oz* starring Liza Minnelli was Filmation's first full-length feature. How did the project get initiated?

PRESCOTT: It was a logical continuation if you ever wondered what happened to Dorothy after her visit to Oz. She wanted to go back and visit old friends. She wanted to see how the Scarecrow was doing now that he had a new position. (Norm reminded me that at the end of the original *Wizard of Oz* movie the Scarecrow was appointed as mayor.) We hired Sammy Cahn and Jimmy Van Heusen to compose the music. Judy Garland signed the contract for Liza, who was sixteen. We still have Liza's contract.

TBSOOL: Were there any plans for an *Oz* spin-off series?

PRESCOTT: We wanted to do a spin-off series, but we never got around to it.

TBSOOL: What do you think of the new school of animators, writers, etc.?

PRESCOTT: I admire talent who are creative and clean. I don't like dirty. You shouldn't expose kids at an early age to the things you'd expose to adults. We had a training program at Filmation. We hired writers, twenty-one- and twenty-two-year-olds, straight out of college. Some of them stayed with us for a couple of years, including Sam Simon (executive producer and writer of *The Simpsons*), Don Bluth (*Rock-A-Doodle*), Tim Burton (*Batman, Batman Returns, Beetlejuice, Family Dog*), and John Kricfalusi (*The Ren & Stimpy Show*).

On a personal note, while it was actually another animation studio that inspired me to open the door to the fascinating world of animated cartoons, Filmation was responsible for taking my initial inspiration to an entirely new level. For me, and the global television audience, Filmation's cleverly designed circular logo (the logo spun around like a wheel, which enabled the viewer to read Norm and Lou's names twice) would automatically symbolize innovative and exciting television. The studio and the partnership were true class acts.

While Norm didn't offer any particular formula for his successful career, he did say he enjoys his free time, "playing golf and playing with computers." In closing Norm said, "The next decade will be even more exciting and will introduce new innovations never before seen. Therefore, I never look back. Be a part of tomorrow."

## COMMENTARY ON CHAPTER 10: AN INTERVIEW WITH NORM PRESCOTT

Norm Prescott described the company's "long relationship" with DC Comics. As producers, Norm Prescott and Lou Scheimer worked with DC on many projects off and on from 1966 to 1981. *The New Adventures of Batman* debuted on CBS in 1977 during the midseason at the same time that Batman and Robin were appearing on Hanna-Barbera's *All New Super Friends Hour* over on ABC. The Filmation production marked the first time that Batman and Robin appeared on two separate productions and networks simultaneously.

I also had a brief conversation with longtime Filmation director Hal Sutherland around September 1990. Hal was working as a consultant on

FOX's *Peter Pan and the Pirates* series, overseeing scripts to ensure that FOX's version of *Peter Pan and the Pirates* stayed clear of any references to the Disney theatrical version of *Peter Pan*. It was the perfect gig for Sutherland, who started his career working on such Disney features as *Peter Pan* and *Lady and the Tramp*.

When I inquired about the competition between Filmation and Hanna-Barbera, he kept saying over and over that Hanna-Barbera had deep pockets, which made me laugh out loud! Looking back, our brief conversation was a missed opportunity because I should have asked Hal about the Filmation character and production designers and his team of Filmation directors, who started their careers animating theatrical shorts, including Anatole Kirsanoff (Warner Brothers), Rudy Larriva (UPA and Warner Brothers), Amby Paliwoda (Disney), Don Towsley (Disney and MGM) and Lou Zukor (Fleischer Studios).

# ELEVEN
# FOX'S SATURDAY MORNING AND SILLY SNEAK PEEKS

Creative freedom was boundless during the early '90s. Cable television was offering viewers new director-driven cartoons. The independent syndicated market was strong. Universal Studios launched a new cartoon division, and a new player, Saban Productions, made its indelible mark in the kids' marketplace. The upcoming chapters are a good sampling of animated and live-action series that I think were successful in capturing what viewers wanted to see in the first half of the 1990s decade.

During the 1990s, I felt that all the networks were just going through the motions in terms of promotion and branding of their respective Saturday morning schedules. When FOX television got into the Saturday morning game, the network brought a freshness to Saturday morning promotion and branding that was lacking on the other networks. Led by network president Margaret Loesch, FOX created a great destination for kids to enjoy Saturday morning programming. Listed below is my enthusiastic review of why FOX television rocked, as well as reminiscing about the Saturday morning sneak peeks.

## TBSOOL EPISODE #0909, SEPTEMBER 1993

And the winner is the hungry FOX television network for bringing back the creative and competitive element that was so lacking on Saturday morning television. During the final weeks of the 1992–1993 season, up-and-coming FOX was nipping at the heels of veteran and season winner CBS. I predict that FOX will win the 1993–1994 season hands down, because unlike the other networks, FOX treats their Saturday morning lineup like stars! Each show and cast gets the ultimate buildup and star treatment. In fact, some of FOX's Saturday morning stars, including Bobby (*Bobby's World*), Buster (*Tiny Toons*), and Super Dave (*Daredevil for Hire*), have enjoyed much of the 1992–1993 season, poking fun at the television networks.

FOX's educational fillers (informative messages that are sandwiched between the cartoon and live-action entertainment) include the inspirational and positive respect and individuality music videos. The Art Smart fillers introduce viewers to the arts and encourage children to explore their creative energy. John Walsh (host of FOX's *America's Most Wanted*) is also part of the FOX filler team, playing host and chaperon to *The Totally for Kids Club*. The members of the club discuss crime prevention tips and nutrition. In addition, club members stage exercises to demonstrate how viewers can protect themselves against strangers and would-be kidnapers.

When I feverishly watched Saturday morning television as a child, there was one undisputed king of Saturday morning programming: CBS (1966–1973). By 1974, CBS's hot streak was over, and the network found itself fighting for programming dominance. Going for the quick fix, CBS purchased a total of six new shows. In addition, CBS made plans to produce a sneak-peek special. Traditionally, sneak peeks were designed to give kids and parents a preview of the new Saturday morning programs. After actress Hope Lange hosted one of the first sneak-peek specials back in the fall of 1969 on ABC, NBC and CBS followed suit, until all the networks figured out that sneak peeks didn't guarantee big ratings.

For CBS's sneak-peek moment, the network hired the Hudson Brothers to host the gala event. Joining the Hudson Brothers at Television City were other CBS stars and the Jimmy Dale Orchestra. Suddenly, the sneak-peek special resembled the network's other top-rated, big-budgeted musical-variety program, *The Carol Burnett Show*. While bouncing down a long white staircase and wearing white tuxedos to match, the Hudson Brothers sang "Socko Saturday" during the finale. The scene was hilarious, classic, and so memorable.

# COMMENTARY ON CHAPTER 11: FOX's SATURDAY MORNING AND SILLY SNEAK PEEKS

### *1993 FOX Saturday Morning Lineup*

FOX's dominance and on-air personality was reminiscent of CBS's Saturday morning heyday, when the network dominated by producing enthusiastically great Saturday morning promotions and proud voices singing in harmony "Saturday morning on CBS!"

The entire on-air personality of the FOX network, from a psychology standpoint, radiated confidence, which I believe translated to viewers and later to ratings success.

### *The Hudson Brothers*

While the Hudson Brothers did a good job presenting the new shows of the 1974–1975 season, *The Hudson Brothers Razzle Dazzle Show* only lasted one season. Still, I have to give it to CBS because having the Hudson Brothers host the sneak-peek special was a brilliant idea and a great way to introduce the musically talented brothers to a kids' audience. I also like the fact that CBS spared no expense for the sneak-peek special. I shouldn't be too surprised; CBS didn't get the nickname "Tiffany" for producing on the cheap.

Other noteworthy items from the 1974–1975 season include *Shazam!* The live-action adventures of Captain Marvel was a big winner for CBS. The debut of *Land of the Lost* from Sid and Marty Krofft Productions landed solid ratings for NBC. Hanna-Barbera's *Hong Kong Phooey* won viewers for ABC. The 1974–1975 season also marked the end of the Archies franchise, which up until the 1974–1975 season was CBS's ace in the hole, consistently generating high ratings for the network. *The Archies* was also one of the few shows that received full episode orders every season. Undaunted, Filmation Productions sold *The New Archie/ Sabrina Hour* to NBC during the 1977–1978 season. Unfortunately, the series only lasted one season.

# TWELVE

# KING ARTHUR AND THE KNIGHTS OF JUSTICE

*King Arthur and the Knights of Justice* caught me by surprise. I really liked this show from the start. It didn't hurt that I was a fan of Jean Chalopin, who created *Jayce and the Wheeled Warriors*, a syndicated action-adventure show launched in 1985. While I was never a fan of the original King Arthur story, the premise of this animated series was intriguing. The newsletter below captures the greatness of the series.

## TBSOOL EPISODE #0707, JULY 1993

Characters from King Arthur's court were always popping up in the issues of *Diana Prince, The New Wonder Woman (*DC Comics, 1969). During one such adventure, King Arthur's nemesis, Morgana, was accidentally transported from her castle to New York's lower east side. Morgana befriends some neighborhood folks (hippies), drop-kicks Diana, and marches onward to conquer New York City. A few years later, Morgana was stirring up trouble for Filmation's *Freedom Force*, whose members included Merlin, Isis, Hercules, Sinbad, and Super Samurai (CBS, 1978).

Currently (in the sixth century), Morgana is at the top of her game in the animated production of *King Arthur and the Knights of Justice*. Written and produced by the talented Jean Chalopin, this weekly syndicated program put a new spin on King Arthur's story. In the first episode, titled "Opening Kick-Off," we learn through Merlin that Arthur and his knights have been imprisoned by Morgana in the "cave of glass."

With Arthur out of the way, Morgana's horde of warlords (led by Lord Viper) attempt to take control of Camelot. Anticipating that Merlin will use his magic to protect Camelot, the warlords distract the old magician, which allows Warlord Black Wing to swoop down and abduct his intended victim, Queen Guinevere. Left with few options, Merlin uses his magic to search the endless timelines of the future. His mission: to seek honorable and temporary replacements for Arthur and the others.

The sorcerer's powerful magic travels through time and space, selecting the Knights football team, whose star quarterback is named (what else) Arthur King. King and the entire team are transported back in time to Camelot, where Merlin explains the situation. The once confident football team is somewhat wary and overwhelmed in their new surroundings, but they come to the understanding that their own timelines might be affected if Camelot is allowed to fall. Each week brings new experiences as Arthur and his teammates become a cohesive fighting unit against the warlords.

In Chalopin's animated version, we are allowed to see the several roles that Arthur plays as monarch. He is first and foremost King Arthur of the roundtable, leader and hero to all. Arthur is also a king of the people who is readily available for an audience. He is both a teacher and a friend who advises and sets examples for the squires, who someday hope to become knights themselves.

*King Arthur and the Knights of Justice* could easily be categorized as just another sword-and-sorcery series; however, the battles with the warlords are balanced by the beauty of Camelot. With its lush gardens and exquisite landscaping, Camelot looks more like a wonderful weekend getaway than a battlefield. In fact, there is beauty in almost every inch of this animated series. Queen Guinevere and her ladies in waiting are gorgeous. Arthur King and the knights are dashing and handsome. The costuming is brilliant, and the overall art, scenery, and backgrounds are soothing to the eye.

As for the villain, or in this case villainess, Morgana is heartless, ruthless, cunning, and above all, smart. She desires total domination and is not about to take a backseat as your typical medieval wench of the day! While most of the story's focus is on Arthur, Morgana's motives for injustice are just as fascinating. Unfortunately, we never get to find out how Lord Viper and the other warlords are "made out of stone." Still, the squires, Everett, Tyrone, and Sir Breeze (one of two African Americans who have been stranded in Camelot), as well as Sir Darren, Sir Lance (Lancelot), Lady Elaine, Sir Tone, Lady Mary, and Sir Wally, make up a diverse group of interesting characters.

## COMMENTARY ON CHAPTER 12: KING ARTHUR AND THE KNIGHTS OF JUSTICE

*King Arthur and the Knights of Justice* became a strong contender in the competitive syndicated market thanks to Chalopin's creative touches, which included a great premise, exceptional storytelling, and beautifully drawn animated characters.

During this period, I discovered another Jean Chalopin production titled *The Bots Master*, which was syndicated in 1993. *The Bots Master* chronicled the adventures of robotics inventor Ziv "ZZ" Zulander's fight against an evil corporation determined to use intelligent AI robots to take over the world. *The Bots Master* would have been a welcomed pick for the original newsletter, but unfortunately I just didn't have the time to write a review for the series.

# THIRTEEN
# MIGHTY MORPHIN POWER RANGERS

I had so much fun writing this tongue-in-cheek review, which I thought was appropriate since the tone of the *Power Rangers* series was very tongue-in-cheek. *Power Rangers* filled a live-action superhero void that had been missing from kids' television. The creation of *Power Rangers* also helped FOX Kids solidify their programming strategy.

## TBSOOL Episode #23, March, 1994

I heard a terrible rumor the other day that the United States government will no longer send disaster relief funds to the city of Angel Grove, California. Why? Because Angel Grove has depleted their disaster relief funds in a war with a mystic named Rita Repulsa (voiced by Barbara Goodson). Rita, you see, is pissed off and wants revenge on Zordon (David Fielding), who imprisoned her more than ten thousand years ago. Instead of flying her broom to New York and causing havoc (Rita doesn't have a broom but should), she chooses instead to invade little Angel Grove as her test invasion city. Zordon quickly finds six teens with "attitude" to defend Angel Grove. Thus, Earth's new defenders, the Power Rangers, are born.

Unless you've been living under a boulder, *Power Rangers* is FOX television's number-one children's series. The show has combined the popularity and action of the best Bruce Lee movies with those cheesy but popular Godzilla films. The lucky actors playing the Power Rangers are Austin St. John (Jason, the Red Ranger), Thuy Trang (Trini, the Yellow Ranger), Walter Jones (Zack, the Black Ranger), Amy Jo Johnson (Kimberly, the Pink Ranger), and David Yost (Billy, the Blue Ranger), and playing Tommy, the long-lost Green Ranger, is Jason Frank.

When these kids get a chance to relax, they attend school and work out at the Angel Grove Gym and Juice Bar. The series has been compared to the *Transformers* and *Ultra Man* (because the Rangers have the ability to morph Godzilla size with their power Zords), but the real appeal of these strutting, clean-cut, dinosaur-powered heroes is action! One of the Power Rangers's greatest battles took place when the Green Ranger (Tommy) became one of Rita's rouges. After making quick work of Zordon (Tommy banished the leader to the outer limits of the galaxy), he promptly destroys the Rangers's power Zords and, per Rita's agenda, causes mayhem, hysteria, and chaos for the citizens of Angel Grove (it was great)! By the end of the battle, the besieged and battle worn Rangers are ready to bag it, but they wisely choose to come back swinging.

The supporting players Bulk and Skull (Paul Schrier and Jason Narvy) serve as the Power Rangers' antagonists at school (those poor kids just don't get a break). I'm sure the audience loves Bulk and Skull, but their attempts to be funny seem forced. Besides, who needs Bulk and Skull when there's Rita Repulsa guzzling down the scenery like cheap champagne? Rita's Norse god getup, perfectly capped teeth, and alien-invading dialogue, "I'm so bad," (despite her lip-synching ability) makes her the new cheesy camp champ. When the battle is over, the obligatory moral of the story stuff is substituted with Rita wailing like Lucille Ball, stating, "I've got a headache."

The proud parents of the *Power Rangers*, Haim Saban and Shuki Levy, made their first impression in the animation biz as musical composers, arrangers, and lyricists for DIC Enterprises, Filmation Productions, and Jetlag Productions. Over the years, Haim has concentrated on running Saban Entertainment, while Shuki has served in his new role of executive producer and is one of the best song writers and composers in the business. Levy's musical arrangements for *Power Rangers* fit the personality of the series; however, he manages to slip in some hard-driving funk backgrounds for all those school dance scenes. Perhaps for the first time since his *Kidd Video* days, the songwriter-musician gets to let his rock-musician hair down. Bravo! Go go Power Rangers!

## COMMENTARY ON CHAPTER 13: MIGHTY MORPHIN POWER RANGERS

The *X-Men* series was actually FOX's number-one series. *X-Men* catapulted FOX from the number-three network to the number-one network and created the official big bang of the 1990s, similar to the events of CBS's big bang of the 1966–1967 season. While many *X-Men* series have come and gone over the years, I consider the Saban-produced *X-Men* series the best of the best in terms of accurately capturing the spirit of the *X-Men* comic series. The ratings from *X-Men* firmly put the FOX Kids Network on top as the ratings leader, which allowed the fledgling network to take its rightful place as the prominent industry leader of the 1990s.

New versions of *Power Rangers* continue to be produced, and the brand is officially evergreen. During the series's early success, a traveling live-action show was produced so that kids could see the Power Rangers "live." Parents waited in long lines to get *Power Ranger* toys since none of the stores could keep the popular toys on the shelf. *Power Rangers: The Movie* was released in 1995 and proved a financial success despite mixed reviews. In 2001, Saban created Saban Capital Group, Inc., which specializes in media entertainment and communication industries.

# FOURTEEN
## DOUG

When Nickelodeon started airing *Doug* at 7:00 p.m. on weeknights, I watched the series every night, taking my usual notes in preparation for this newsletter. My sudden interest in *Doug* and obvious change of viewing habits puzzled my son Jomar, who inquired, "Daddy, don't you like *Hard Copy* anymore?"

## TBSOOL EPISODE #24, APRIL 1994

My first impression of Doug was that of an older, latter-day Charlie Brown—a loser. *Doug*, however, proved to me that you can't judge the hood by its decor. If you haven't tuned into *Doug* or don't know his story, here's the deal: Doug Funnie lives in the fictional town of Bluffington, USA, and like FOX TV's Bobby (*Bobby's World*) and HBO's Martin (*Dream On*), viewers get to preview Doug's thoughts and fantasies. While I enjoy Bobby's anything-is-possible adventures and Martin's quick-as-an-eyeblink thoughts, some of Doug's fantasies take center stage for entire episodes. In addition, his day-to-day adventures are preserved in a journal.

The series also employs an interesting beginning, middle, and end format, which hasn't been used in children's television for years. The first scene usually focuses on the conflict of the story, but it isn't necessarily where the story actually begins. Next, Doug and Porkchop (his faithful, scene-stealing dog) introduce the title of the story (e.g., "Doug Can't Dance"). Since the viewer has already seen what the beef is all about, Doug reintroduces the story with a voice-over: "It all started ...," etc.

Doug's fantasy characters, Smash Adams (a James Bond type) and Quailman (a Superman type who comes off more like Underdog), help Doug solve real-life adolescent problems. He often asks himself, "What would Smash Adams do?" Somewhere between fantasy and reality, Doug comes up with a solution.

Doug's parents (Phil and Theda) are regular folks, but like most kids, Doug thinks his parents are lame. His older sister, Judy, is a nouveau Shakespearean actress who you wouldn't dare call a wannabe. His best friend, Skeeter Valentine, can always be counted on for support and kookiness. And at eleven and a half years of age, Doug has a romantic interest named Patti Mayonnaise, whose folksy, down-home charm would win any boy's heart. Rounding out the cast is Roger Klotz, who plays the resident antagonist of the series. Roger's smart mouth, slick smile, and threatening fiery-orange hair keep Doug and the series from becoming too cutesy. Doug has a solid relationship with his neighbor, Mr. Dink, an adult and mentor to Doug whose quirky king-of-the-gadgets style and nerdy personality could have easily been exploited into a Dennis the Menace-Mr. Wilson relationship. Fortunately, Mr. Dink is respectable and is readily available whenever Doug has a problem (which is often).

When Mr. Dink invites Doug to go fishing, he finds out that he's been "suckered" (as Roger put it) to help Mr. Dink catch "Chester," the fish that got away. Doug wants to abandon ship, but because it's important for him to do the right thing, he sticks it out, and the fishing trip ends on a positive note. While I know this sounds predictable, Doug isn't perfect. He lets most situations get the better of him (when his heart starts pounding and the sweat begins cascading down his face, watch out!) Still, it's Doug's open mind, positive energy, and perseverance that make him unique and likable. In fact, the episodes are played out like mini parables, where the moral of the story and the characters don't have to be explained every minute.

The opening theme music and background arrangements were created by Fred Newman. The music is a great representative of the new school of musicians who are having a good time shaping the musical styles and relationships with the animated cartoon. Newman's mouth-beat rhythms and congas are a distinct and noticeable asset to the production. The series has had many great musical moments (Porkchop's hip-hop rap, "Everybody Do the Dog," and "Killer Tofu," sung by Doug's favorite rock band, the Beets) showcase Newman's musical diversity and spirit. Synchronization between music and character is at its most subtle and wickedly best during the scenes when Judy is explaining "the theater" to Doug. Newman's jazzy flute-bass-beatnik style combined with Judy's "I'm an actress" performance is so cool.

## COMMENTARY ON CHAPTER 14: DOUG

*Doug* premiered on Nickelodeon during the 1991–1992 season and featured new episodes through the 1994–1995 season. A new version of *Doug* was created in 1996 when ABC bought the rights to creator Jim Jinkins's company, Jumbo Pictures, and secured the rights to *Doug*.

# Fifteen
# THE NEW SPEED RACER

## TBSOOL Episode #25, June 1994

Despite its plot gaps, limited animation, and over-the-top voice-overs, Tatsuo Yoshida's *Speed Racer* (syndicated, 1967) remains the all-time favorite CJI (classic Japanese import) among viewers. While I believe fans would be skeptical of any new version of *Speed Racer*, Fred Wolf's version (coproduced with Speed Racer Enterprises) is currently being viewed by a target audience who know little or nothing of the classic version. *Speed*'s new scripts have been written by David Wise, whose talents and zesty writing style worked magic for Wolf's other hits, *Teenage Mutant Ninja Turtles* and *James Bond Jr.*

For starters, Wise introduces Speed's true costar, the rugged red, white, and blue Mach-5 racing car with an exterior made out of an indestructible alloy. In addition, the Mach-5 has a wind resistance factor of zero, hyperturbo afterburners and autojacks. Pops Racer, the genius behind the Mach-5 and Speed's father, is portrayed as a patient and pragmatic businessman—a departure from his earlier characterization, which depicted the inventor as an overzealous, impatient loudmouth. However, when mutants from the future try to steal the Mach-5, Pops springs into action and takes charge, which is something his counterpart from the classic version would definitely do.

Sprite, Speed's incorrigible little brother—along with Sprite's pet chimpanzee, Chim-Chim—fueled the original *Speed Racer* with much-needed comedic relief and naughtiness. These days, he's respectful to his father and big brother Speed, but his funky attitude is gone, and so is his prominence in the story line. It makes one wonder why his part wasn't just written out entirely. At least the creative team got Spritle and Chim-Chim out of their matching twin jumpsuits. Yuck!

Speed's female friend, Trixie, looks totally unrecognizable as a blonde. Trixie's break-out-the-bleach look comes as no surprise, since female cartoon characters get modified just for the heck of it more often than their male counterparts. Could there be sexism in the world of animation? Trixie is independent and one of the boys, which means she must keep a cool distance between herself and Speed. Translation: Speed doesn't have time for any hanky-panky with Trixie because the situation will inevitably slow down the story line.

Sparky, the talented mechanic who played second and third fiddle to Spritle and Trixie in the old days, has been bumped up to Speed's buddy and confidant. Speed's relationship with Sparky works perfectly, since both are about the same age and love cars and racing. In the old version, Speed wouldn't talk to or confide in anyone (his older brother, Rex, wasn't around thanks to Pops.) So if Speed had a problem, he would simply talk to himself through a voice-over.

Of course it just wouldn't be the new Speed Racer if the mysterious Racer X wasn't on board to give Speed some well-deserved competition. According to legend, Speed's older brother, Rex, ran away from home, only to reappear on the race scene again as the mysterious Racer X. He cleverly keeps his identity a secret because he wants to prove to Pops that he can be the best race car driver in the world (plus his dual identity serves as a cover for his espionage work). As a result, Racer X cannot allow himself to be close to Speed. Speed, on the other hand, feels instinctively close to Racer X but doesn't know why.

The new Speed Racer is a cool dude; he's likable, but he's no longer the rebel or monolithic figure of the past. He's been watered down to the boy next door who saves the world but doesn't get the girl.

## COMMENTARY ON CHAPTER 15:
## THE NEW SPEED RACER

My review of *Speed Racer* wasn't exactly optimistic. Looking back, I wanted the new version of *Speed Racer* to be exactly or close to the original series.

# SIXTEEN
# EXOSQUAD

MCA/Universal Family Entertainment and Universal Cartoon Studios Division were launched by Jeff Segal in 1991. *Exosquad* was chosen as the series to capture the 1990 programming trend that combined adventure, science, and robotics. The plight of an enslaved Earth being held captive by a genetically engineered Neosapien leader named Phaeton and the *Exosquad* team that battles to win Earth's freedom captured me as a viewer.

## TBSOOL EPISODE #26, SEPTEMBER 1994

In order to meet the technological and physical demands of the Venus/ Mars colonization effort, Dr. Kav Maginus breeds thousands of genetically engineered, superior human beings called Neosapiens. The Neos, whose biological construct is completely null and void of human emotion, become the perfect workers. It is only a matter of time before the Neosapiens demand the same rights as their human masters; that sparks a bloody rebellion on Mars. Seventy-nine years later, 2119 AD, a Neosapien leader named Phaeton (governor and general of the United Martian Commonwealth) devises a calculating plan of deceit, revenge, and conquest.

Phaeton executes the financial component of his secret plan by "looting" the Martian treasury. Next, the dynamic leader sweeps into the General Assembly of the Home Worlds and interrupts the heated debate on whether the Home Worlds should start a war with the space pirates (the pirates attacked an unarmed ship). Phaeton, the diplomat, gives a speech that is both intelligent and pragmatic. He convinces the Home Worlds to chase down Simbacca and his band of space pirates and assures the overwhelmed crowd that the Neosapiens will support their efforts.

Enter Lieutenant J. T. Marsh, the commanding officer of Able Squad, who along with the rest of the fleet has been ordered to crush the pirate threat. Before the first laser cannon can be fired, the commanding officers buck for power and position. Captain Marcus, an old-school military strategist who is hungry for war and glory, bullies Admiral Winfield into making the wrong moves against the enemy. Marcus is also opposed to J. T. and the use of their E-Frames (robotic battle armor). By the time the fleet catches up with the pirates and battles it out on the moons of Saturn, communications between the fleet and Earth are mysteriously cut off. The Exotroopers soon learn that Earth, Mars, and Venus have been attacked by the Neosapiens, led by Phaeton.

As the fleet journeys back to Earth (leaving Simbacca and the pirates for another day), the trooper's hopes and fears are revealed. Lieutenant Nara Burns is concerned about her family on Venus (in later episodes she is reunited with her brother, James, who has become a resistance fighter). Marsala, the only Neosapien Exotrooper in the fleet, becomes a convenient target of Captain Marcus. The Exotroopers arrive on Earth and find their cities destroyed and their family and friends dead, missing, and being held as prisoners of war.

Citizens who haven't been captured accuse the Exo Fleet of abandoning them to chase pirates. One of the supporting characters, a cheesy television personality named Amanda Conner, plays ball with the Neosapiens because she wants to keep her television job. (I thought Conner's situation was an accurate portrayal of shifting politics). Meanwhile, Amanda's ex-boyfriend, Sean Napier, a former Exotrooper and soon-to-be-fired police officer, gets rescued by one of the many resistance forces on Earth. When Napier crosses paths with J. T., the two strong-willed individuals become unlikely allies against the Neosapiens.

The Exotroopers have no special powers or abilities (funky haircuts, definitely). The series doesn't feature any scene-stealing aliens or mushy romance, although sparks were flying between Marsala and Nara.

*Exosquad*'s story moves a bit slow, but the pacing is justified by the detailed subplots and endless characters (e.g., Exotroopers, resistance fighters, collaborators, Neosapiens, and pirates). The production is well executed, well written, and beautifully animated. Segal and his team of new school talent have done a great job developing an action series that is first-rate. Peace.

# SIXTEEN 1/2
# EXOSQUAD

*Will Meugniot, Creative Director and Producer of Exosquad, Comments on Season Two*

I had the pleasure of talking to Will Meugniot on the phone back in September 1994. Listed below were some of his comments regarding season two.

"Second and third-generation cartoonists are getting control of the product" is how Will Meugniot assesses the industry and the success behind *Exosquad*. He adds, "Universal has been very supportive in letting us do something different." *Exosquad* will be seen five days a week this season with the addition of "thirty-nine new half hours," which Meugniot says "looks good."

Will has more than sixteen years experience in both the animation and comic book worlds and agreed to give TBSOOL the scoop on what will happen during *Exosquad*'s second season. He confirmed, "There will be an alliance with the pirates and Exotroopers." Will also provided a shocker: "One of the major Able Squad guys is going to die." Meugniot mentioned something about the "conclusion of the war" but because he did not want to give anything away, details were sketchy.

## COMMENTARY ON CHAPTER 16.5: EXOSQUAD

Fifty-two episodes of *Exosquad* were produced. I recently watched the season one DVD, and the series still holds up, which is a testament to the creative team who worked on the *Exosquad* series.

# SEVENTEEN
# THE TOMORROW PEOPLE

## TBSOOL Episode #27, October 1994

Billed as Nickelodeon's first sci-fi adventure series, *The Tomorrow People* delivers the goods with a cast of young actors who play likable, spiritual, and smart characters. Shot exclusively in London, *The Tomorrow People* stars Kristian Schmid (Adam), Christian Tessier (Megabyte), and Naomie Harris (Ami). *The Tomorrow People* can mentally teleport themselves to any part of the world. They can heal the human body and possess telepathic abilities.

When Adam, Megabyte, and Ami come together to thwart international espionage and terrorism, *The Tomorrow People* are born. In their first adventure, Adam emerges from the ocean fully clothed and disoriented. He is mysteriously attracted to a gothic figure in the sand. Upon closer examination of the figure, Adam is sucked into what he discovers to be a crashed alien spaceship. Adam learns that the ship serves as a beacon to alert people like himself who have reached the next stage of human evolution—a Tomorrow Person. Meanwhile, Megabyte and his friend Kevin (Adam Pearce) use a moving city bus to blast unsuspecting citizens with their superpowered water guns. When Megabyte invites Kevin to spend the night at his house, the two boys experiment with Kevin's telepathic ability. Somehow the alien ship taps into Kevin's telepathic signals, which leads to Kevin and Megabyte discovering that they are both Tomorrow People.

The US Scientific Intelligence Authority and the British Department of Scientific Intelligence join forces to investigate the teleporting teenagers. Leading the task force is Megabyte's dad, General Damon (Jeff Harding), who hasn't a clue that his own son is a teleporter, or that his errant colonel is planning to sell the Tomorrow People to the highest bidder. What follows next is mayhem, threats, and plenty of running around, which prepares the kids for their next opponent—Dr. Culex.

Actress Jean Marsh guest stars as the brilliant Dr. Culex, who has been kicked out of legitimate scientific circles because of her nut-job experiments. Undaunted, the doctor continues her experiments and creates a breed of killer mosquitoes. She cooks up a plan to steal a device that can genetically engineer millions of her "babies." When Kevin gets bitten by one of the mosquitoes, Dr. Culex kidnaps him because he's "seen too much." I like the fact that trouble usually finds the Tomorrow People rather than the other way around.

Kristian Schmid plays Adam with maturity and mystification, while Christian Tessier brings complexity to Megabyte's seemingly laid-back personality. Naomie Harris gives Ami all the girl-next-door virtues but quickly lets the audience know there's a tiger in her tank. The special effects employed on this series aren't exactly over-the-top, but the scripts and performances make you forget what's lacking. Roger Damon Price, the creator and writer of *The Tomorrow People*, brings a down-to-earth feeling to the teleportation and the physical and spiritual worlds that boils over into the entire production.

## COMMENTARY ON CHAPTER 17: THE TOMORROW PEOPLE

I believe that with the creation of *The Tomorrow People*, Nickelodeon was going after the same audience that propelled FOX's *Power Rangers* to ratings heights. *The Tomorrow People* proved successful and rode the wave of adventurous teenagers defending life, liberty, and freedom (even if it was across the pond).

# EIGHTEEN
# DONOVAN COOK'S 2 STUPID DOGS

The funniest and scariest thing about *2 Stupid Dogs* is the fact that we all know people like them. The little dog (Mark Schiff) reminds me of one of my father's friends, replete with anxiety and a foaming-at-the-mouth approach to life. The big dog (Brad Garrett) resembles my barber and sounds like singer Barry White (not that Barry White is stupid).

While the current crop of animated comedies has gone the Tex Avery, over-the-top, gross-out route, *2 Stupid Dogs* achieves great comedic heights with simplicity and subtlety. During one hilarious episode titled "Family Values," the two stupid dogs get adopted by the antimatter Brady Bunch of their world. When the big dog's paw catches on fire during the Bradys' out-of-control barbecue, he slowly opens his mouth, and in his slow-as-a-mole deadpan style delivers the line that brings down the house: "Ow!" Donovan Cook, the creator and director of *2 Stupid Dogs*, happily takes the Brady joke even further by poking fun at Filmation Productions' animated music videos of *The Brady Kids*. In Cook's musical rendition of "Sunshine Day," the Brady's jalopy is substituted with an out-of-control lawn mower, and with the *2 Stupid Dogs* on board, the Brady kids sing the off-key "Lawn Mower Day" song and crash!

The stupid dogs are homeless. They go from alleyways to department stores to Las Vegas and will work for food. Getting food or not serves as the conflict in the dogs' lives. Food is seen as the ultimate, almost unobtainable object. One such food search leads the dogs to their first of many encounters with eyeglasses-so-thick Little Red Riding Hood. Red invites the dogs to Grandma's house for cheesecake, and mistakes the big dog for Grandma, which leads the big dog to ask, "What's a grandma?" Since the stupid dogs don't know where they're going and Red is blind as a bat, they end up at the three bears' funky pad, bypassing Grandma's house. When the bears return home and notice that somebody's been drinking out of their toilets, they confront the trespassers and demand that Red hand over the coveted prize—the cheesecake. The dogs and Red gulp down their cheesecake, and the bears go for broke. When the dogs run into Red again in the pivotal episode "Red Strikes Back," the little dog tells her off: "The last time we went with you, we got beaten up by bears with plungers!" Of course they go with her again, because they are two stupid dogs.

Everyone's favorite *2 Stupid Dogs. 2 Stupid Dogs.* Licensed
By: Warner Bros. Entertainment Inc. All Rights Reserved.

Lending support to *2 Stupid Dogs* is Hollywood (Brian Cummings), who has the unfortunate task of playing most of the supporting guest roles in the series. Hollywood is the new Elmer Fudd, despite his Sam Kinison delivery: "Isn't that cute? But it's wrong!" During one episode, Hollywood mistakes the dogs for stunt monkeys for hire. A few hundred takes and union breaks later, the dogs demolish the studio and get offered their own series by an executive who looks suspiciously like Fred Seibert, the president of Hanna-Barbera. Donovan Cook's *2 Stupid Dogs* is a clever intellectual comedy and perfectly showcases the new-school talent at Hanna-Barbera Productions. My only complaint is that the series comes on too early in the morning (a shocking 7:05 a.m. on Sundays on TBS). Peace.

## COMMENTARY ON CHAPTER 18: DONOVAN COOK'S 2 STUPID DOGS

Donovan Cook was on my original mailing list, and when he read the *2 Stupid Dogs* newsletter, Donovan sent me the following note.

Donovan Cook

*2 Stupid Dogs* is a good representation of a creator and director-driven cartoon series. The new-school talent that worked on *2 Stupid Dogs* went on to develop many creator and director-driven hit series of their own, including Genndy Tartakovsky (*Dexter's Laboratory* and *Samurai Jack*), Craig McCracken (*The Powerpuff Girls* and *Foster's Home for Imaginary Friends*), and Seth MacFarlane (*Family Guy*).

# NINETEEN

# THE ALL-STAR SATURDAY MORNING HALFTIME REPORT

Once the Saturday morning schedules were set, the networks didn't tweak the schedules too much, and for the most part, the series that viewers were watching in the fall had a good chance of being around by the end of the season. However, by the late '70s, network executives started making aggressive programming moves that were similar to prime time. The network schedules were tweaked, and in some cases new programming such as *The New Adventures of Batman* replaced rating-challenged programming during the 1976–1977 midseason. These next chapters will discuss the '90s Saturday morning programming strategy, along with spotlights on Saturday morning series, specials, and my personal favorites—comic books, Ted Nichols, and the *BraveStarr* series.

## TBSOOL EPISODE #29 AND #30, JANUARY/FEBRUARY 1995

The first half of the 1994–1995 television season has been thrilling and fiercely competitive. Animated programs have never looked better, and for the first time in many years, there is an abundance of quality live-action programs for children. Thanks to FOX, Saturday morning is competitive again. Before FOX got into the Saturday morning game, ABC wasn't spending much on show promotion, and CBS's promotions were just okay. TBSOOL accurately predicted that FOX would win the 1993–1994 season. As it stands right now, FOX's diverse take-no-prisoners schedule has the edge over CBS, while ABC can only hope for a decent third-place finish.

ABC and CBS need to do a better job promoting their Saturday morning lineups. ABC has the most diverse schedule, but it needs to build its veteran shows, including *Sonic, Cro,* and the timeless *School House Rock* shorts. ABC also needs to promote its new shows, which include *ReBoot* and *Bump in the Night.* CBS should invest some real cash in *WildC.A.T.S.* and *Skeleton Warriors.* Most of FOX's programs *(The Adventures of Batman & Robin; X-Men; Eek! The Cat; The Terrible ThunderLizards; Jim Henson's Dog City)* are no longer new, which means FOX better get busy and build its new stars like *Carmen Sandiego* and *The Tick.*

# THE SATURDAY MORNING SCHEDULE AS OF JANUARY 28, 1995

| Time Slot | CBS (Network) | FOX (Network) | ABC (Network) |
|---|---|---|---|
| 8 a.m. | Disney's The Little Mermaid | Jim Henson's Dog City | Sonic the Hedgehog |
| 8:30 a.m. | Beethoven | The Mighty Morphin Power Rangers | Free Willy |
| 9 a.m. | Disney's Aladdin—The Series | Animaniacs | Tales from the Cryptkeeper |
| 9:30 a.m. | Teenage Mutant Ninja Turtles | Eek! The Cat/The Terrible ThunderLizards | ReBoot |
| 10 a.m. | WildC.A.T.S. | The Adventures of Batman & Robin | Bump in the Night |
| 10:30 a.m. | Skeleton Warriors | The Tick | Fudge |
| 11 a.m. | Garfield and Friends | X-Men | The Bugs Bunny & Tweety Show |
| 11:30 a.m. | | Where on Earth Is Carmen Sandiego? | |
| Noon | Beakman's World | Local programming | Cro |

*8:00 a.m.*

The working relationship between puppet-artist-animator Eliot Shag and the toon star of *Jim Henson's Dog City*, Ace Hart, is engaging. Eliot and Ace don't always agree on stories, plots, or gags, which creates many spontaneous comedic situations. *Jim Henson's Dog City* is currently doing battle against the very popular and beautifully animated *Sonic the Hedgehog. Sonic,* who I consider the new Road Runner with an attitude, is quickly becoming the veteran anchor of ABC's schedule. However, ABC should promote *Sonic* as a true adventure series. I'm not crazy about *Disney's The Little Mermaid* series. (I always thought Saban's version was better.)

*8:30 a.m.*

The Mighty Morphin Power Rangers' arch enemy, Rita Repulsa, has been banished, and her replacement, Lord Zedd, doesn't possess any of Rita's campy comedic virtues. I'm bored with the *Power Rangers*. I liked the original cast. The new Rangers look so much alike, they could be interchangeable. Moving right along, I never liked the *Beethoven* movies, but the series is entertaining. *Free Willy* is the '90s version of Hanna-Barbera's *Moby Dick* except Willy actually talks. *Free Willy* and *Beethoven* are similar in the sense that both series boast sincerity, friendship, and loyalty. (The colorful beachfronts on *Free Willy* and the great landscaping on *Beethoven* don't hurt.) Will *Beethoven* and *Free Willy* end up as the sacrificial lambs of *The Mighty Morphin Power Rangers*? Stay tuned.

*9:00 a.m.*

*Animaniacs* is an outrageous, decadent comedy that I think is being wasted on kids. The series achieves that old-school Warner Brothers flavor along with a singing cast. The boy-next-door *Disney's Aladdin—The Series* is predictable. *Tales from the Cryptkeeper* (based on HBO's popular series *Tales from the Crypt*) isn't scary. If *Tales from the Cryptkeeper* had been syndicated, I believe audiences would have seen a much scarier production.

*9:30 a.m.*
*Eek! The Cat/The Terrible ThunderLizards* is one of the best underrated comedies on the air right now, but ABC's surreal computer animated series *ReBoot* is a strong contender. *ReBoot* features excellent over-the-top graphics and decent stories, and it is the best series on ABC's schedule. CBS moved the hyped-up adventure series *Skeleton Warriors* to the 10:30 a.m. slot and placed the eternal *Teenage Mutant Ninja Turtles* to duke it out with *Eek!* and *ReBoot*. I predict that *Eek!* and *ReBoot* will get renewed and that *The Teenage Mutant Ninja Turtles* will be seen exclusively on the USA's Cartoon Express.

*10:00 a.m.*
*Bump in the Night*'s clay animation characters possess great personalities and spunk but may get lost in the battle between *WildC.A.T.S.* and *The Adventures of Batman & Robin*. *WildC.A.T.S.* (based on the best-selling comic book series) is impressive, but the animation is stiff compared to other animated action series. Still, the *WildC.A.T.S.* is holding its own against the Emmy award-winning *Batman* series.

*10:30 a.m.*
*The Tick* provides viewers with quality over-the-top scripts that adults enjoy but will probably send the kids to the competition. My son Jomar watches *The Tick*, but he doesn't get the jokes and has no idea where the story is going. He prefers to watch *Skeleton Warriors*, which has all the guts and glory that *The Adventures of Batman & Robin* could use. *The Addams Family*, which was recently yanked by ABC, was replaced on January 14 with the live-action comedy *Fudge*. The true battle will be between *The Tick* and *Skeleton Warriors*.

*11:00 a.m.*
Going into their third season, the *X-Men* will easily win the time period with an overabundance of episodes this season. Could it be that FOX has been hoarding episodes? If you compare the animation from the first season to what the *X-Men* series looks like today, you would swear that all the X-Men had plastic surgery (which is a good thing).

*The Bugs Bunny & Tweety Show* shorts are classics that can be seen seven days a week in syndication, but the series still manages to find an audience on Saturday morning. (Variations of the franchise have been renewed consistently since 1968.) *Garfield and Friends* is the comedy veteran anchor of the CBS lineup. *Garfield* employs all my favorite old-school sound effects and gags, and he's a good-for-nothing scamp. Since the *X-Men, The Bugs Bunny & Tweety Show*, and *Garfield* are all classics, expect all three to return for the 1995–1996 season.

*11:30 a.m.*
*Where on Earth Is Carmen Sandiego?* is the best-written animated series of its kind to feature a woman as the star and mastermind. She's slick, inventive, and a female James Bond who knows how to work technology and her trench coat with vigor. *Carmen Sandiego* educates and entertains with great graphics and educational tips, but FOX needs to build *Carmen Sandiego* an audience and keep the preemptions to a minimum.

*Noon*
*Beakman's World* is a funky version of *Ask Mr. Wizard*, while *Cro* educates viewers through his prehistoric adventures. When *Beakman's World* graduated from syndication to network status, the series lost its popularity and audience in the process. *Cro*, which got beat up by *Jim Henson's Dog City* and *Disney's The Little Mermaid*, should perform better in the noon slot, but leave it to the networks to pit two educational programs against each other. Peace.

# TWENTY
# COMIC BOOK MADNESS!

Comic book conventions are great because it's the one place where fans can clearly see how the comic book world and the animation world are so intertwined. There's more going on at comic book conventions than just great comic books for sale. There's collector art; gaming; and comic book/television panels that feature famous artists, writers, and actors from the comic book, animation, science fiction, and television worlds. However, the big draws are the media exclusives, where movie studios and television networks feature sneak peeks at upcoming movies or television pilots. Comic book conventions should be retitled as media conventions because the conventions feature a little bit of everything that is associated with pop culture and the media.

## TBSOOL Episode #32, May/June 1995

During the month of February, I attended a comic book convention in New York City. I limited myself to only buying $150 worth of books, and I found plenty of collectable items. I purchased *Teen Titans #26* (featuring the first appearance of Mal, who would become the first African American Teen Titan). I obtained the rare Whitman Book adaptations of *Fat Albert and the Cosby Kids* and *The Harlem Globetrotters*. I found *The Justice League of America #75* (featuring Black Canary's official induction into the League). I dug up *Lois Lane #99*, which featured a catfight between Lois and Lana Lang over Superman (priceless and hilarious). I also picked up *Adventure Comics #399* starring Supergirl that introduced the first African American characters to the story line, Johnny Dee and Roxie.

I discovered Dan Parent and Bill Golliher's fabulous circus folks, *The Carneys #1*. Dan and Bill are representative of the new-school artists and writers who are emerging from Archie Publications under the leadership of managing editor Victor Gorelick.

Some convention folks spent many hours in long lines trying to get their favorite artists to sign their books, while others (like myself) bum-rushed the convention workers to obtain free posters, books, etc. Marvel Comics had the best free stuff! I did, however, obtain the signature of legendary Archie Publications artist Dan DeCarlo. The Hanna-Barbera artists copied Dan's famous drop jaw, as well as Dan's other trademark facial expressions, when the studio worked on *Josie and the Pussycats* almost twenty-five years ago. And speaking of Josie, the video pirates were at the convention, supplying bootleg old-school copies of *Josie and the Pussycats*, Krofft's *H. R. Pufnstuf* and *Lidsville*, Filmation's *Justice League*, Hanna-Barbera's *Moby Dick* (spelled Mobey Dick), and many other Saturday morning favorites. DC Comics attracted mobs of people by providing a sneak preview of *Batman Forever*. (Most folks gave it a thumbs-up.)

Notable no-shows included Milestone and Vertigo, whose books are distributed by DC. Perhaps Milestone and Vertigo were near the DC Comics table?

Surprises included running into Dwayne Ferguson, creator, writer, and artist of the best-selling comic book *Captain Africa*. Unlike most superhero fare, *Captain Africa*'s adventures take place outside the United States (in Egyptica, Africa to be exact). Ferguson has combined African traditions and history with high-tech, no-holds-barred action.

A few feet away from Dwayne, I met Reggie Byers, who is the creator, artist, and writer of *Kidz of the King*. The superpowered multicultural Kidz, (Truth, Mercy, Faith, and Zeal) are young ambassadors of the King (Jesus Christ). The Kidz teach and preach the ways of the Lord in the hood. I told Reggie that old-school television producer Lou Scheimer had worked on a similar animated project with the Seventh-Day Adventist Church. And speaking of Lou Scheimer, he reported to TBSOOL that the great Filmation film library he built with Norm Prescott, Hal Sutherland, and many other great talents has been "acquired" by Hallmark. On May 2, during a phone conversation with TBSOOL, Hallmark Entertainment confirmed the acquisition of the Filmation library.

## COMMENTARY ON CHAPTER 20: COMIC BOOK MADNESS!

*Dan Parent*

I had the pleasure of meeting Dan Parent at Comic-Con in 2009, and we talked about *The Carneys*. He seemed pleasantly surprised that I remembered that book, which was just a one-shot deal.

*The Filmation Library*

The Filmation library was acquired by Hallmark Entertainment, as indicated in the above newsletter. The Filmation library is currently owned by DreamWorks Animation.

# TWENTY-ONE
# THE TOP TEN SHOWS FROM THE 1994–1995 SEASON

When we look back at series such as *ReBoot* and *Where on Earth Is Carmen Sandiego?*, we can see that the networks and studios were embracing the emerging digital technology to get a leg up on the competition. *Where on Earth Is Carmen Sandiego?* boasted a high-gloss look and graphics and, along with *ReBoot*, pushed networks' budgets to new highs, which I think was a good development. *Spider-Man: The Animated Series* made its debut on FOX Saturday, February 4, and along with some of the series listed below, *Spider-Man: The Animated Series* boasted computer-generated backgrounds as well. The following list was picked based on ratings dominance and creativity. And while I didn't always have the ratings reports at my fingertips, the shows below were proven winners.

## TBSOOL Episode #33, July/August 1995

*#1 ReBoot (ABC)*
Billed as the first 100 percent computerized animated series, *ReBoot's* greatest assets (other than the compelling computer-generated imagery and great 3-D animation) are the characters. Bob (the Guardian), Dot, and Enzo (the good guys) appear almost perfect. However, we find Dot to be a little controlling, Enzo a bit wild and impetuous, and Bob a bit cocky. Compared to the grandiose style of the villains (Megabyte and

Hexadecimal), the good guys seem normal. If the creative team hadn't developed these complex and likable characters, the 3-D stuff wouldn't have held up for a minute.

Every Saturday morning, viewers get to see Bob, Dot, Enzo, Frisket (Enzo's dog), and their friends (Phong, Mike the TV, and miscellaneous computer sprites) defend their home Mainframe from the machinations of Megabyte, the chaos of Hexadecimal, and the uncertainty of the games sent in by the User. *ReBoot* has booted every program CBS and FOX has thrown at it, and it is computer noir at its finest.

### #2 Bump in the Night (ABC)

I thought this program was going to get killed in the ratings by *The Adventures of Batman & Robin* on FOX and *WildC.A.T.S.* on CBS. However, Mr. Bumpy, the star of *Bump in the Night*, beat up the action heroes. This series has a wonderful cast of characters and has heralded the return of clay animation to Saturday morning television. Mr. Bumpy is a cross between James Brown and Daffy Duck. Bumpy's cohorts include Squishington (a sky-blue glob of clay) and Molly Coddle (a huggable comfort doll). These three diverse friends share adventures in "the boy's" room when the boy is asleep. *Bump in the Night* leaves viewers with a warm, wonderful feeling (a rarity on Saturday morning). Besides wrecking "the boy's" room at night, the characters appear in the Karaoke Cafe music segments, which pay homage to the grand finale musical variety shows of the past.

### #3 Where on Earth Is Carmen Sandiego? (FOX)

How does one describe Carmen Sandiego? She's brilliant. She's resourceful. Her crimes are just short of magnificent. Carmen's high-tech getaway gadgets and smooth, confident demeanor overflow with star quality. While Carmen remains "wanted," only a few select people from the Acme Detective Agency (Ivy, Zack, and the Chief) and an adolescent PC interactive Player are privy to her global crime spree. Unlike the usual superhero types, Ivy and Zack must rely on their knowledge of geography, history, and language in order to track and capture the elusive Carmen Sandiego. The Player exchanges bon mots with Carmen through his computer and helps Zack and Ivy find clues from the crime scenes. The computer-generated imagery mixed with the legendary live-action guest stars is great! *Where on Earth Is Carmen Sandiego?* inspires and stimulates its audience to use their brain power in a very clever and entertaining manner. At the twenty-second annual daytime Emmy Awards, *Where on Earth Is Carmen Sandiego?* won an Emmy in the category of outstanding animated children's program (1994–1995 season).

## #4 Animaniacs (FOX)

It would take an entire episode of TBSOOL to describe why *Animaniacs* is a winner. It's as if the creative team sat down and said, *"Tiny Toons* is great, but if we had to do it all over again, what would we do differently?" The headliners of *Animaniacs*—Yakko, Wakko, and Dot—are funny, cute, crazy, wicked, and slick, but most of all, they are incorrigible. Some of the other stars of the show, Slappy Squirrel, the Goodfeathers, Pinky, and the Brain seem to be cut from the same old-school Bugs Bunny cloth of comedy. Every gag, joke, and comedic gesture pushes the envelope with no apology. The "wheel of morality" segment is a slap in the face to the network executives who avail their authority on television producers to insert message segment bumpers at the end of their programs. *The Animaniacs* don't seem to learn anything from the wheel of morality. Oh well. At least viewers get to share a big laugh.

## #5 The Tick (FOX)

Created by Ben Edlund and adapted from the comic book series, *The Tick* is completely uncouth. The Tick lacks skill and smarts, and he can be a pain in the neck. If the Tick wasn't so bothersome, this series wouldn't be so entertaining. The Tick has a sidekick named Arthur who in the first episode leaves his ho-hum accountant job to become a crime fighter. (I'm still trying to figure out how Arthur manages to pay his rent.) The Tick and Arthur fight crime in what looks like New York City (it's not). The villains (Chairface Chippendale and Mr. Mental), are crazy, campy, and over the top. The superheroes (American Maid and Die Fledermaus) bicker at a moment's notice. The resident television newscaster reports the Tick's exploits in a slow, matter-of-fact monotone style is subtle and hysterical.

## #6 Spider-Man: The Animated Series (FOX)

The friendly neighborhood *Spider-Man* is back on Saturday morning television, boasting great animation and stories. Per the agenda of Stan Lee (*Spider-Man's* cocreator and executive producer), the series introduces viewers to Spider-Man's early days as a misunderstood hero. Spider-Man delivers plenty of zingers and action as he takes on the Lizard and Venom, who makes his first animated appearance. *Spider-Man* is so likable and familiar to viewers, how could this series fail?

### #7 Garfield and Friends (CBS)

Who would have known that a couple of prime-time specials featuring Jim Davis's obnoxious cat, Garfield, would lead to the longest-running comedy on CBS's Saturday morning schedule? *Garfield* remains popular with viewers on both network and syndicated television because the creative team has consistently cranked out great gag scripts. Viewers love to see Garfield being rude, crude, and rebellious, as well as funny, resourceful, and subtle. The supporting toon players, Jon and Odie, are the perfect window dressing for Garfield, the self-indulgent, fat, greedy, lasagna-eating star. The U. S. Acres farm animals hold their own in their separate adventure and music segments. If *Garfield* challenged the other greedy cartoon stars in an all-out eat-a-thon, we could only guess the outcome. However, if the challenge was based on ingenuity, imagination, and ruthlessness, we all know who would win that battle. *Garfield* is a quadruple Emmy award winner. No wonder he's got a big ego, or is it a big appetite?

The cast of *Garfield and Friends* ham it up! From left to right: Binky the Clown, Penelope, Nermal, Garfield, Odie, Jon, and Dr. Liz Wilson. © Paws. Used by permission. All Rights Reserved.

## #8 X-Men (FOX)

Since its dramatic debut during the 1992–1993 season, *X-Men* has been consistently well written, delivering well-rounded characterizations and nonstop action. Some critics tried to trash *X-Men* because of the violence, but I can cite many episodes that focused on the emotion, tears, anguish, passion, and love that the X-Men have demonstrated toward each other and humankind. Other than the syndicated adventure series, *Exosquad*, no other action-adventure series comes close to pushing the dramatic emotional envelope seen on the *X-Men* series.

## #9 The Mighty Morphin Power Rangers (FOX)

Adults are sick of *Power Rangers*, but let's face it: this series is a legitimate hit. Thanks to high ratings, popularity, and gusto to boot, *Power Rangers* have practically vanquished the watchdog groups who say the show is too violent. In addition, Saturday morning's live action-adventure genre, which was dead (the Krofft production of *Land of the Lost* notwithstanding), is back with a vengeance. The success of *Power Rangers* has brought good publicity and respect to Saturday morning television. Now, if we can only get the networks to order more than thirteen episodes per season.

## #10 The Bugs Bunny & Tweety Show (ABC)

When CBS decided to combine the *Bugs Bunny* and *Road Runner* shows into *The Bugs Bunny and Road Runner Hour* during CBS's championship Saturday morning 1968–1969 season, "No more rehearsing or nursing a part. We know every part by heart" (lyrics from the opening theme song), has translated into twenty-six years of the absolute best classic comedy cartoons on Saturday morning. While the Road Runner no longer headlines the show with Bugs Bunny, Tweety, as the replacement headliner, has not slowed down this ratings powerhouse. The gang from Warner Brothers can been seen on TNT, Nickelodeon, TBS, and in syndication; however, *The Bugs Bunny & Tweety Show* still manages to find an audience, which is a testament to these wonderful classic characters. Bravo!

# Twenty-Two
# TRIPLE PLAYS

Ratings determine the life cycle of a series. A typical life cycle of a Saturday morning show back in the day was two years. However, as broadcast networks have moved toward creating their own studios and series ownership, the programming owned by the networks seem to last longer than the programming in which the networks didn't necessarily have a financial stake.

## TBSOOL Episode #34, September/October 1995

A triple play occurs on Saturday morning television when three competing shows in the same time slot get the boot (are canceled). One such triple play took place during the 1994-1995 season with the cancellations of *Jim Henson's Dog City* (FOX), DIC's *Sonic the Hedgehog* (ABC), and Disney's *Little Mermaid* (CBS). All three shows battled it out at 8:00 a.m., and all three got the boot!

The first Saturday morning triple play I can recall took place during the 1974–1975 season with the cancellations of *The Hudson Brothers Razzle Dazzle Show* (CBS), the animated *Star Trek* (NBC), and *The Super Friends* (ABC). All three programs shared the time slot of 11:30 a.m., and all three series got the boot!

The 1994–1995 battle started with CBS and FOX playing possum with their Saturday morning schedules. Eventually, the posturing subsided, which resulted in a fast-and-furious battle complicated by FOX, ABC, and CBS maneuvering their schedules every time you blinked.

*Jim Henson's Dog City* (FOX) became a midseason casualty, while

*Cro* (ABC) and *Sonic the Hedgehog* (ABC) were both gone by summer. ABC's *Bump in the Night* held its own against FOX's hot midseason entry, *Spider-Man: The Animated Series*.

CBS's hyped-up *WildC.A.T.S.* fizzled but was picked up by the USA Network. *Where on Earth Is Carmen Sandiego?* (FOX) occupied more time slots than any other series on the schedule. *ReBoot* (ABC) became the breakaway hit of the 1994–1995 season, while *Garfield and Friends* (CBS) and *The Bugs Bunny & Tweety Show* coasted to easy victories. *The Teenage Mutant Ninja Turtles* (CBS) was renewed despite rumors that the show was finished.

FOX won the overall 1994-1995 ratings race in spite of their veteran shows and few new hits. ABC's second-place victory came as a surprise (undoubtedly helped by *ReBoot*, *Bump in the Night*, and ABC's midseason live-action entry, *Fudge*). CBS finished in third place.

Will FOX remain number one? Will ABC steal the ratings crown from FOX? Will *The Mask* rescue CBS from ratings obscurity? I can only tell you that the 1995–1996 season (already in progress) is going to be a doozy. Stay tuned.

## COMMENTARY ON CHAPTER 22: TRIPLE PLAYS

NBC dropped out of the Saturday morning game in 1992 and created a Saturday version of the *Today Show*. I think *Jim Henson's Dog City* was too sophisticated for kids. *Cro*, on the other hand, was pro-educational, and educational shows didn't get high ratings on Saturday mornings, especially when kids were probably watching PBS (which isn't ratings driven). *Sonic the Hedgehog* was one of the best-selling game properties of the early 1990s, but the television franchise seemed to be losing steam by 1995.

# TWENTY-THREE
# 'TWAS THE NIGHT BEFORE BUMPY

TBSOOL EPISODE #36, DECEMBER 1995/JANUARY 1996

Mr. Bumpy, the clay animation star of *Bump in the Night* stars in his first holiday special. Suitably titled *'Twas the Night before Bumpy*. The ninety-minute special unfolds when Mr. Bumpy hatches a scheme to go to the North Pole to hijack some of Santa's Christmas presents.

While Mr. Bumpy and Squishington can maneuver themselves around "the boy's" house, going to the North Pole proves to be a challenge. The pair end up in Peru, where they are held captive by a campy earthworm (voiced hilariously by actor-comedian Cheech Marin). The crazy clay twosome leave Peru and arrive at the North Pole just in time to encounter Kung Fu chopping elves and snowmen. Despite their setbacks, Mr. Bumpy and Squishington encourage each other and complain to each other through holiday songs. ("Jingle bells, Bumpy smells," etc.) If you are not familiar with *Bump in the Night*, this Christmas special would be a great opportunity to see one of the best Saturday morning shows on the air in full effect. Peace.

## COMMENTARY ON CHAPTER 23: 'TWAS THE NIGHT BEFORE BUMPY

The fact that ABC ordered a ninety-minute *Bump in the Night*–themed Christmas special proves how much faith the network had in the series. Unfortunately, as the next chapter will reveal, *Bump in the Night* will get caught up in the crosshairs of network politics, which will derail the beloved series.

# TWENTY-FOUR

# THE 1995—1996 SATURDAY MORNING RACE GETS BRUTAL!

## TBSOOL EPISODE #37, JANUARY/FEBRUARY 1996

In a move not seen since the early days of Saturday morning programming, the ABC network canceled most of their Saturday morning lineup. While many good programs got the ax, I am confident that some of ABC's casualties (*Dumb and Dumber, What-a-Mess, ReBoot,* and *Bump in the Night*) will resurface on one of the rival networks. *Dumb and Dumber,* for instance, would make a great companion program for *2 Stupid Dogs* on the Cartoon Network. Still, some of ABC's shows deserved the boot. I don't think anyone was watching *Free Willy,* and as for the irrepressible and annoying *Fudge,* good riddance! *Winnie the Pooh,* which replaced *The New Adventures of Madeline* in the beginning of the season, also received its walking papers.

*The Bugs Bunny & Tweety Show* and *The ABC Weekend Special* survived the cancellation slaughter. I believe ABC will never cancel *The Bugs Bunny & Tweety Show* for fear the rival networks will scoop up the veteran series. The forgettable *ABC Weekend Special* survived by being politically correct and pro-educational. I also believe ABC's programming strategy would have played out differently if Disney (ABC's new corporate parent) wasn't in the picture.

## COMMENTARY ON CHAPTER 24: THE 1995—1996 SATURDAY MORNING RACE GETS BRUTAL!

As expected, with the acquisition of the ABC Network, Disney created and added a few new Disney programs to the schedule. Thanks to the acquisition of Jumbo Pictures, the studio that produced the original *Doug* series, the new version of *Doug* titled *Brand Spanking New! Doug* premiered on the Disney-owned ABC Network during the 1996–97 season. Other Disney additions included *The Mighty Ducks* and *Gargoyles: The Goliath Chronicles*. By 1997, ABC's Saturday morning block was rebranded as Disney's One Saturday Morning. *The Bugs Bunny & Tweety Show* finally left the ABC Network and Cartoon Network became the exclusive home of the entire *Looney Tunes* library.

# TWENTY-FIVE
# TED NICHOLS— MUSICAL MASTER

As musical director for Hanna-Barbera Productions, Ted Nichols' music would define the Hanna-Barbera sound. Ted told me during an interview on March 27, 2014, that "I really started at H-B in spring of '63 but wrote most of the cue music for *Jonny Quest* in the fall of '62, and then the Flintstone Christmas music, which I don't think I got any credit for, but it did open the door because the music editors liked what I did."

Indeed, many of his memorable opens and background music tracks can be heard on *Jonny Quest, The Herculoids, The Fantastic Four, Scooby-Doo*, and *Josie and the Pussycats*. After he left Hanna-Barbera in 1972, Ted composed his first opera, which was based on *Pilgrim's Progress* (1977). The opera premiered in Helsinki, Finland. Being the consummate composer, writer, and lyricist, Nichols wrote all the music as well as the dialogue for *Pilgrim's Progress*. Ted Nichols has not slowed down; he continues to compose and write music for various projects. Ted Nichols' musical scores for *The Fantastic Four* and *Josie and the Pussycats* are great examples of his musical genius and virtuosity as a composer.

## TBSOOL Episode #38, March/April 1996

Ted Nichols' exciting musical opening for *The Fantastic Four* combines classical jazz with touches of the big band sound. His fine trumpets, piano, saxophone, and flutes crescendo dramatically into one of his trademark musical eruptions that finishes off the opening theme perfectly. Since *The Fantastic Four* battled the forces of evil in New York, Ted created a jazzy laid-back arrangement using a piano, clarinet, and acoustic guitar, which embodied the cool, sophisticated streets of New York. I was most impressed with a musical piece that employed a flute to convey the psychological complexity of these great Marvel heroes. All the music had a New York jazz, East Village vibe that made every scene of *The Fantastic Four* work.

Dressed for success. The cast of *The Fantastic Four* take a night off from fighting crime and appear in their civilian identities. From left to right: Johnny Storm (the Human Torch), his sister, Sue Richards (the Invisible Woman), Ben Grimm (The Thing), and Reed Richards (Mr. Fantastic). Licensed By: Warner Bros. Entertainment Inc. All Rights Reserved.

In my opinion, no other series in the history of Hanna-Barbera was as musically driven as *Josie and the Pussycats*. While Nichols created new music for the series, his musical tracks from *Jonny Quest*, *Shazzan*, and the *Herculoids* were used to give Josie credibility as an action-adventure star. In an episode titled "The Great Pussycat Chase," a background track from Nichols' *Arabian Knights* is mixed into newly composed background music that fades into the *Josie and the Pussycats* single "Together," which is performed by the band aboard a luxury liner. The sequences in which the background music interacted with the Pussycats' rock-blues and funk singles provided the audience with mini background concerts and made the series a joy to listen to and watch.

Ted Nichols' music tracks complemented the rock-blues and funk singles for the cast of *Josie and the Pussycats*. From left to right: Alexander, Josie, Melody, Valerie, Alan, Alexandra and Sebastian. Licensed By: Warner Bros. Entertainment Inc. All Rights Reserved.

## COMMENTARY ON CHAPTER 25: TED NICHOLS—MUSICAL MASTER

I had a chance to catch up with Ted Nichols and talk to him about his wonderful Hanna-Barbera career.

> *The Best Saturdays of Our Lives*: It's an honor to talk to you. I grew up watching a lot of cartoons and listening to your music. I've been a fan for a long, long time.

Ted Nichols:  You poor guy!

TBSOOL:  (*Laughter*) The Internet has so much misinformation, and it's a little confusing. I have a lot of the Hanna-Barbera DVDs as well. I reread the article that I came across and e-mailed the reporter, who was nice enough to contact you on my behalf. In the article it says that you started writing themes for *Jonny Quest*?

TN:  Let me tell you, *Jonny Quest* was the first open that I wrote for; the main melody was already written, and I was actually [working] at a big church in LA. I don't know if you've ever heard of J. Vernon McGee? He was the pastor at that time, when I was with him in Los Angeles. [The church] was a mega church before they knew what a mega church was. I was the minister of music there, along with being director of bands at Cal State University of Los Angeles. I did a whole lot of writing for the church and getting big groups, you know, since I was right there close to Hollywood. Anyway, one of the animators from Hanna-Barbera came in and started singing with my choir. He liked what I did, and so I was just kidding with him and said, "Why don't you introduce me to your boss?" The next week, I get a call from Bill Hanna.

TBSOOL:  Wow!

TN:  He said, "Can you have lunch with me?" And so I went to have lunch with him, and he said, "We are working on a new series called *Jonny Quest*, and I'd like you to write some cues for that, and if we like 'em, we'll see." So the next week, I started writing cues because the melody was already written, for the theme, and so I just took parts of the melody and wrote a bunch of stuff for the scenes. They liked it and said, "Hey, come back. We'd like you to do some more. In fact, we've got a Christmas show, a *Flintstones* Christmas show. Would you like to write for that?" And I said, "Well, twist my arm a little." (Chuckle). Shortly after that, Bill and I got to be good friends, and he said, "Well look, we are going to need someone full-time, and we would like to have you do it." So that was 1962 when I first started writing, and I stayed with them until 1972.

TBSOOL: I wasn't sure when you left [Hanna-Barbera]. I just knew that there was a change in the music. As a kid growing up, I realized that things were a little different.

TN: I guess. It's just my style.

TBSOOL: You composed music for a lot of action shows: *Space Ghost*, *The Herculoids*, *Young Samson*, and *Shazzan*.

TN: What happened with Hanna-Barbera, with some of those shows, I forget how many, they got some of the guys in Hollywood who were already writing hit tunes to do some of the theme songs, and then I would go ahead and write the rest of the music. I did the hard part because I would have to do all the timing on the shows, write all the cues. In fact, there is one that you may not know: *The New Adventures of Huck Finn*, which was a combination of animation and live-action. That was one that I wrote the original theme, that and *Josie and the Pussycats*. Listen, I did about thirty or forty. I really don't remember all the ones I did because what I had been doing in the meantime, I had written about five operas because I'd rather write that kind of music than just cartoon stuff, although I enjoyed writing the cartoon music because it was challenging. You had to write to the second. Most all the shows that you mentioned, I wrote most all the music.

TBSOOL: I like the music for *The Fantastic Four*. It seems that for that particular show, you were going for a definite New York music sound of the '60s. A kind of beatnik style, jazzy sound. It was very different than a lot of the other music you composed at Hanna-Barbera.

TN: Well, I'm glad you like that. I remember when I first found out about [*The Fantastic Four*], I wrote a couple of themes for it, and it was the first time I was using what they call a theremin. It had a different kind of sound. Anyway, yeah that was fun.

TBSOOL: The opening theme song for *The Fantastic Four* is very robust and very strong. I read a lot of Marvel comic books, and I just felt like that opening theme was just really perfect for *The Fantastic Four*.

TN: Well, thank you. I appreciate that. What usually happened on a show was I'd meet with, of course, Bill. He ran the shop. Joe did a lot of PR stuff and worked with a lot of the people in Hollywood, but Bill and I worked together because Bill ran the shop there mostly. Anyway, what we would do, Bill would call in the guys that were going to work on [the shows] as the animators and producers of that particular series, and we'd all talk and look at storyboards. Then I'd go to a studio and write several cues, record, bring 'em back with me, and meet with the same guys, and they'd say, "Oh yeah, this is what we like," and so that's how we would get the themes for the shows.

TBSOOL: I had sent you a list.

TN: Do you have the music or the shows themselves?

TBSOOL: Yes, on DVD.

TN: You might look and see if my name is on those. I think one of the last shows I wrote was *Scooby-Doo*.

TBSOOL: *Josie and the Pussycats* is one of my favorites in particular because I was really shocked by the direction that Hanna-Barbera took with the show. The stories in comic books were really geared toward girls, and the fact that Hanna-Barbera decided to make Josie and her friends action stars really threw me as a kid, and then your music was just perfect for the series. I like the fact that you mixed in cues from your other shows like *Jonny Quest*.

TN: If you ever went to Hanna-Barbera, you would see a whole room with different cues that I wrote for all the shows, and the music editors are the guys that decided, "Oh, I like what he wrote in this show, and it would work fine for this scene," and that's how it got in there.

TBSOOL: If you were the main composer for the series and the music editors had to pick your cues, they would never mix your cues with somebody else's, would they?

TN: No. I guess the union might get on them [music editors] if they did something like that. I would be a very rich man had I still gotten royalties for those shows. I had to sign everything over to Hanna-Barbera. The only show I ever got residuals on was *The Man Called Flintstone*, which was a full-length feature, and I did get some royalties from that. My last check from ASCAP was something like $6.25. That's a laugh! But that's okay. God has been good to me, and I can't complain.

TBSOOL: That's wonderful. I feel blessed just to be talking to you. On some of the websites, they give you credit for the *Jonny Quest* music, and on others the credit is given to Hoyt Curtin.

TN: Hoyt and I are good friends. When I resigned in '72, then I think they got Hoyt back again. Hoyt's a good guy, and he did write all the things prior to my coming.

I really respected Hoyt because he was there before I was and felt kinda bad that they didn't call him as full-time musical director, but Bill liked what I did, so I was there.

TBSOOL: I think as a composer you really delivered. I believe that someone should have given you a special Emmy award for all the amount of work you put in for all those shows.

TN: It takes so long. I sit down with the music editor that was in charge of doing that particular show [*Jonny Quest*], and he and I would count frames, and I'd make notes on my music paper to make sure that I had the exact frame run. If somebody got hit [visually], I had to hit them music-wise, and then seeing the different scenes, I'd write the music for that.

TBSOOL: Around the time I was watching *Josie and the Pussycats*, I started taking piano lessons. I started to understand how music played a part in a cartoon series, and I never looked at cartoons the same way again.

TN: I did it for so long, I sort of took it for granted. But hey, you don't sound like where you're calling from. (I was calling from Atlanta, Georgia.)

TBSOOL: I'm originally from New York.

TN: I thought so. I was there for the annual meeting of the National Opera Association. I love New York. It's a super place to be.

TBSOOL: Did Bill Hanna decide the creative teams?

TN: For the most part, Bill ran the shop, and he had all the animators working there under him along with his producers, who would follow through for him. In fact, there was a Charles Nichols.

TBSOOL: Yes, I've seen his name in the credits.

| | |
|---|---|
| TN: | Yes, I used to know him pretty well, and he did a lot of the producing for [Bill Hanna]. |
| TBSOOL: | No, relation right? (Laughs) |
| TN: | Actually, my original name was Theodore Nicholas Sflotsos. |
| TBSOOL: | Is that Greek? |
| TN: | My dad was Greek. When I decided to do things in Hollywood, I changed it to Ted Nichols. It's much simpler. |
| TBSOOL: | What exactly is a subtheme? Is the subtheme based on the main theme? |
| TN: | Exactly, you don't want to copy it too close. Some of the theme you can use and add extra notes to fit what you want it to fit for that particular scene. |
| TBSOOL: | Did you know any of the musical directors at the other studios? |
| TN: | I knew some of the guys. Of course, it's been so long ago. It was way back in the '60s. A lot of the guys are gone. All of us were so busy; we really didn't have time to fraternize much. |
| TBSOOL: | I have talked to a lot of people who were making cartoons during the '60s and '70s, and it seemed like the schedules and delivery was crazy. |
| TN: | In fact, I remember one series, the *Huck Finn* series. We sat down with the music editor on Monday and got the timing down. I had to write all the music and get it done and send it to New York before Friday! You learn to write very fast! |
| TBSOOL: | That is extraordinary! |

TN:　　　　　I appreciate talking to you.

TBSOOL:　　Thank you so much for taking the time to talk to me.

Ted Nichols continues to compose music. He told me, "Last spring my fifth opera was premiered in Louisville, Kentucky, and now I am arranging hymns in several contemporary styles for a gal who is doing evangelistic concerts here in the States and in China, and will be doing my opera *Pilgrim's Progress* in England."

# TWENTY-SIX

# LOU SCHEIMER'S BRAVESTARR

*BraveStarr* was the last space Western animated series produced entirely in the United States, and the last series produced by Filmation Productions.

## TBSOOL EPISODE #40, SEPTEMBER/OCTOBER 1996

The opening sequence of *BraveStarr* teases the audience with the sound of galloping horses that are reminiscent of the 1930 radio serials. An old saloon piano can be heard clearly in Frank Becker's musical score. And finally, when *BraveStarr*'s logo is branded across the universe, revealing New Texas for the first time, the sequence pays homage to one of the greatest television Westerns of all time: *Bonanza*.

Originally syndicated during the 1987–1988 season, BraveStarr was the first Native American animated character to headline a futuristic Western epic. Set in the twenty-third century on a planet called New Texas, trouble arrives with the discovery of Kerium, a rare red crystal that can power starships and weapons. Settlers, prospectors, miners, merchants, and outlaws descend on the planet, much to the dislike of the native Dingo gangs, who loathe humans. Anarchy, lawlessness, and turmoil soon become a way of life on the Kerium-fever-ravaged planet. The space marshals step in and dispatch one marshal to bring law and order to New Texas—Marshal BraveStarr.

Instilled with spiritual animal powers (ears of the wolf, eyes of the hawk, speed of the puma, and strength of the bear), BraveStarr's quest for peace and justice are supported by a diverse group of characters that cleverly display the diversity of New Texas' citizens. Shaman is a healer, mystic, and spiritual leader, and is also BraveStarr's mentor. BraveStarr's partner, Thirty/Thirty, is a techno horse who chews up the scenery and whose smart remarks ("I like a well-armed enemy. Makes the fight last longer") often stole the show. Also mixing it up is J.B., the fiery, gavel-swinging lady judge who spends more time fighting desperadoes than sitting on the bench. Other supporting cast members include Deputy Fuzz of the Prairie People; Doc Clayton (the town doctor); Molly, the stratostage (stage coach) driver who seems to be the endless target of Dingo gang assaults; and Handlebar, the saloon owner whose specialty drink is sweetwater.

On the outskirts of town, Stampede, the oldest evil spirit on New Texas, uses prospector-turned-outlaw Tex Hex to stir up trouble for BraveStarr, Shaman, and the settlers. Tex Hex is your basic low-down crook, kidnapper, thief, and all-around villain who will do anything to obtain Kerium. His gang consists of a bunch of misfits. There's Skuzz, the only cigar-smoking Prairie person to turn evil; Thunder Stick, a robot who talks the talk but can't hit the side of a Turbo mule; Sand Storm, a sand walrus and native of New Texas whose sand breath literally puts people to sleep; and Vipra, a sleek, deadly snake woman who can temporarily paralyze her victims. On the rare days that Tex and his gang take a rest, Dingo Dan, a shape-shifting dingo, and the Krang, a fierce, arrogant interstellar catlike race, provide plenty of trouble for the marshal.

At first glance, *BraveStarr* appears to be a made-to-order Western television fantasy with the perfect leading man and great supporting characters. However, a closer examination of this series reveals that it is a complex mix of perfection, illusion, beauty, majesty, and technology that is heavily grounded in reality. While the series teaches prosocial morals (respect, courage, teamwork, freedom, trust, nonviolence, and the importance of family), the other topics of the series (slavery, temptation, prejudice, and drug addiction) deliver penetrating and unforgettable messages.

One of the best episodes of the series, titled "The Price," is a dark, depressing spiral into the bottomless pit of drug addiction. The episode is written realistically; it pulls no punches and accurately portrays how kids get involved in drugs. "The Price" centers on Jay, a young boy who is talked into trying Spin "because it's fun." The mental high that Jay experiences is handled off screen; however, the physical aspects of Spin are captured dramatically as Jay's eyes roll back, sweat drips from his brow, and his body shakes. In another disturbing scene, Jay mutters to himself in baby talk as he goes through Spin withdrawal.

Still, nothing prepares you for the shocking emotional end when BraveStarr discovers Jay in his clubhouse, dead from a Spin overdose.

Another great episode, "Eye of the Beholder," reveals Tex Hex's origin and how his lust for Kerium turned him into an outlaw. A blind woman named Alli Kingston unknowingly befriends Tex after he is hurt in a battle with BraveStarr. There is a mutual attraction between the pair as Tex reveals to Alli that she reminds him of the woman he left behind for Kerium. Later that day, Tex puts romance on the back burner as he tries to steal the Kerium that Alli is transporting to scientists for research. BraveStarr steps in, a battle ensues, and Tex Hex takes off, leaving his gang to face the marshal. Just as Alli is about to leave town, Tex returns a handkerchief he borrowed from her when he was hurt. She tells him to keep it and adds, "It will remind you of the person who saw the good in you." Alli Kingston departs New Texas, and all seems well until Frank Becker's powerful background music ushers in the scene that captures Tex Hex watching Alli leave New Texas. Tex is slouching slightly. He is holding on to the tip of the handkerchief as it blows in the wind. There are no close-ups of Tex's face, but you feel his pain and regret.

## COMMENTARY ON CHAPTER 26: LOU SCHEIMER'S BRAVESTARR

I think one of the coolest things about TBSOOL episode #40 is the fact that "The Price" and "Eye of the Beholder" newsletter (which were originally published in 1996) made the top five episode list on the *Best of BraveStarr* DVD, which was issued in 2007. In addition, Tom Tataranowicz, who cowrote the "Eye of the Beholder" with M. Stevens, sent me a letter regarding my *BraveStarr* review as well as a copy of *BraveStarr: The Legend* theatrical movie, which was directed by Tom Tataranowicz.

*Mark McCray*

NEW WORLD ANIMATION

TOM TATARANOWICZ
SUPERVISING PRODUCER

November 22, 1996

Dear Mark,

It was nice to speak with you the other day. My Filmation days are filled with good memories and it is gratifying that someone is keeping frequently overlooked and under appreciated projects like "Bravestarr" alive.

In 1986 - 1989, Filmation benefited from the down sizing of other animation studios in town and we accumulated quite a formidable array of talent. For myself, I have gone on the run Marvel Films/New World Animation both creatively and productionwise, with great success for 5 years; Bob Forward is one of the most highly regarded writers in the business; Tom Sito is the head of Story at Dreamworks Animated Features, etc., etc.

The sad thing is that before being shut down, we were doing some extremely nice work like the feature, "Bravestarr, The Legend", "Sherlock Holmes In The 23rd Century" (a Pilot episode down in the "Bravestarr" series), "Bugzburg" and "Bravo" .... all of which were either seen by very few people, if ever indeed shown at all.

Anyway, I am sending you a copy of the "Bravestarr" feature which I directed for your collection. I am quite proud of it and hope you enjoy it.

Thanks again for the newsletter.

Tom Tataranowicz

3340 OCEAN PARK BOULEVARD SANTA MONICA CALIFORNIA 90405
TELEPHONE (310) 581-3200 FAX (310) 581-3290

In 1996, I had no idea the movie existed. *BraveStarr: The Legend* was awesome, as I was able to see how BraveStarr received his animal powers, as well as watch the supporting cast come together for the first time. The movie features great animation, and it would have been cool to see the theatrical feature on the big screen.

Many years later, I had the pleasure of meeting Tom at Comic-Con during one of the He-Man panels in 2006.

Tom Tataranowicz and Tom Sito (who directed "Eye of the Beholder") provided episode commentary for "Eye of the Beholder" on the *BraveStarr Volume 1* DVD release. Tom Sito revealed that the scene where Alli's stratostage leaves New Texas was an "early digital shot that was designed on a computer," and Tom added, "Lou [Scheimer] wanted to go into that new frontier."

After watching the DVD commentary, I contacted Tom Tataranowicz and asked if there were any CGI scenes in the BraveStarr movie.

Tataranowicz said, "There were a handful of CGI scenes in the feature. Primarily, they were machines. The most obvious one I recall is BraveStarr riding an out-of-control 'steed' through a narrow canyon and bouncing off of the walls before ultimately crashing. This is just prior to the origin flashback to Bravestarr's childhood. As you can imagine, the CGI back then around 1987 was fairly rudimentary. The computer animations of the machines were done as a wire frame drawing. Then it had to be cleaned up by hand and the fire added by hand."

In retrospect, receiving Tom's letter and subsequent copy of the movie was a wonderful and unexpected surprise. I'm happy to say that I own the entire *BraveStarr* DVD collection, and right next to that collection is the lone VHS copy of *BraveStarr: The Legend* that was sent to me by Tom Tataranowicz in 1996. Tom Tataranowicz is the president of Gang of 7 Animation/Tom T. Animation.

# Conclusion

When I started *The Best Saturdays of Our Lives* in 1992, I had no idea where the newsletter would lead or what opportunities it would open up for me. I just love the fact that I was able to meet and talk to the talented men and women who created such great television programming. The work of these men and women continues to feed my passion and love for kids' programming, competition, and creativity.

Many aspects of the industry have changed since I started in the business. I watched the dependency of broadcast DigiBeta tape requirements become less important as studios upgraded to digital file delivery. In addition, HD (high definition) has become the standard for broadcast, satellite, and cable operators.

The twenty-four-hour kids' networks have supplanted the traditional Saturday morning broadcast schedules and strategy. In addition, many of the twenty-four-hour kids' networks have gone into business for themselves by creating their own studios, series, online gaming, and toys, as well as partnering with independent studios to coproduce series and specials.

Gone are the days of low budgets and grueling weekly episode deadlines. Premieres of new and returning series are scheduled year-round with special events sprinkled in to capture viewers. Programming can be seen on all screens twenty-four hours a day, including online, mobile, VOD (video on demand), and live video streaming.

It really is a brand-new world, and as a fan of television, I can say that having all these viewing choices is a great convenience.

In spite of the new digital choices, networks are still creating new types of entertainment. Successful shows and trends continue to be spun off. Networks try to duplicate their competitors' successes by creating their own brand of parallel programming. Television ratings still determine if a series will die or live on to renewals and evergreen status.

As I look toward the future of television, with the added value of being able to watch television everywhere, I wait in anticipation for the next big bang that will revolutionize the medium and make every day the best television of our lives.

# INDEX

# B

Bakshi, Ralph, 8, 36

Ball, Lucille, 72

*The Banana Splits Adventure Hour*, 6, 15, 17, 47

Barry, Jeff 17

Bass, Jules, 29

Batfink, ix

Batman (animated), 7, 37, 39, 40

*Batman* (theatrical), 60

Batman and Robin, 7, 20, 37, 60

*Batman Forever*, 102

*Batman Returns*, 60

*Batman: The Animated Series*, 32, 41, 45–46

Bat-Mite, 37

*The Batman/Superman Hour*, 5, 6, 7, 37–39

*Battle of the Planets*, 41

Bay City Rollers, 16

*Beakman's World*, 96, 99

Becker, Frank, 127, 129

*Beethoven* (musician), 52

*Beethoven* (series), 96–97

*Beetlejuice*, 60

The Beets, 77

Bell, Alexander Graham, 30

Bennett, Tony, 55

Berry, Gordon, 58

*Best of BraveStarr*, 129

*The Best Saturdays of Our Lives* (newsletter), xi–xii, xiii, 35, 40, 48, 57, 67, 69, 75, 93, 103, 129, 133

Betty Boop, 52

*Beverly Hills Teens*, 31, 43

Big Seven, x

Billboard Charts, 17

Billy, the Blue Ranger, 72

Binky The Clown, 108

*Birdman and the Galaxy Trio*, 3, 6

*The Biskitts*, 33

Black Canary, 101

Black Manta, 39

Black Vulcan, 37

Blanc, Mel, 24

Bluto, 24, 26

Bluth, Don, 60

Blye-Bearde Productions, 16

Bob (The Guardian), 105–106

*Bobby's World*, 64, 75

*Bonanza*, 127

Bostwick, Jackson, x

*The Bots Master*, 69

*The Brady Bunch*, 19, 25

*The Brady Kids*, 12, 16, 25, 37, 40, 91

The Bedrock Rockers, 16

*Brand Spanking New! Doug*, 116

*The Brave and the Bold*, 39

*BraveStarr*, 46, 95, 127–131

*BraveStarr: The Legend*, 129, 131

*BraveStarr Volume 1*, 131

Brown, James, 106

*The Bugaloos*, 15, 48

Bugs Bunny, 21, 23, 107

The Bugs Bunny and Road Runner Hour, 109

*The Bugs Bunny & Tweety Show*, 96, 99, 109, 112, 115, 116

*Bump in the Night*, 96, 98, 106, 112, 113–114, 115

Burton, Tim, 60

Bustin' Productions, Inc., 32

*Butch Cassidy and the Sundance Kids*, 16

Buzz Saw Girl, 45

Byers, Reggie, 102

# C

# D

Made in United States
North Haven, CT
10 January 2025

64244381R00100